The only treasure

ANN THWAITE

The only treasure

ILLUSTRATED BY GLENYS AMBRUS

BROCKHAMPTON PRESS

By the same author   HOME AND AWAY
THE TRAVELLING TOOTH
THE DAY WITH THE DUKE
(picture book with George Him)
THE CAMELTHORN PAPERS
(Macmillan)

ISBN 0 340 10406 6

First edition 1970
Published by Brockhampton Press Ltd, Salisbury Road, Leicester
Printed in Great Britain by Fletcher & Son Ltd, Norwich
and bound by Richard Clay (The Chaucer Press) Ltd
Bungay, Suffolk
Text copyright © 1970 Ann Thwaite
Illustrations copyright © 1970 Brockhampton Press Ltd

Contents

Riding
Stables

Cottages

FLEUR
BAY

Caves

Pushchair left
here

Jetty

La Falaise

shop

Fleuron Farm

Windmill

- - - - - Footpaths

Lighthouse

HOTEL

Gate

Fleuron Manor

Air raid
Shelter

TO Bonjour Bay

TO ST. HELIER

Empty Cottage

FOR THE KENYONS,
WHOSE HOUSE IT WAS

ONE

Swapping houses

'Are we nearly there? Are we nearly there?' Jenny Simpson chanted over and over again as she bounced about in the back of the car.

'Oh, do be quiet, Jenny. We just don't know,' her mother said. 'They don't seem to go in for signposts here. I've lost track completely.' They were burrowing through green lanes, passing square, flatfaced, shuttered farmhouses with gardens full of flowers, up and down hill. She had a map spread out on her knee.

'Is it Jersey?' Jenny asked.

'Yes, of course it is,' Stephen and Anna said together.

'We came in the plane,' Anna added. 'It was Jersey when we got here. It's all Jersey.' People of three needed lots of explanations. Anna had her finger in *Strangers at the Door*, the book she had been reading on the aeroplane, to mark her place.

Luke Simpson, the father, drove the unfamiliar car gingerly. 'I daren't stop. We might not be able to start again.'

'Well, just crawl next time we see some people, and I'll shout out of the window,' the mother said.

There were some farm labourers sitting in a field, munching bread and cheese.

'Excuse me, we are looking for *La Falaise* – it's a house at Fleuron Bay. Are we on the right road?' The mother spoke quickly and the men looked puzzled, so she started again more slowly. The car stalled and the father swore.

One of the men swallowed his mouthful of bread and nodded vigorously. '*La Falaise? La Falaise – c'est à la gauche*.' He waved his left arm in the air.

Stephen and Anna were talking together again. Jenny repeated her earlier chant. 'What did he say? Was it French? Are we nearly there?' The car jerked as their father tried to start it again.

'You're still in gear,' Stephen said. He longed to take over the wheel.

'All right, all right. I can't find neutral. Why they have to have such crazy gears . . .'

'They probably think ours are,' Stephen said. 'It's just a matter of what you're used to.' He looked rather smug at saying something so reasonable. But his father wasn't listening. He was trying to get into first gear. The car remained firmly in the road opposite the farm labourers, who watched them with interest, curiously.

'They are probably going to report us to the police for having stolen it. They can tell it's not ours,' Stephen said.

'Oh, stupid. It's no use stealing a car in Jersey. You

couldn't get away with it. It's only twelve miles long. I looked it up. And whoever saw a car thief with three children?' Anna laughed at the thought.

'Whoever saw a car thief anyway? You didn't.'

At last the car sprang forward. 'I think I'll stay in first for the rest of the way,' Luke Simpson said. The sweat was pouring down his face. His wife mopped it up gently with her handkerchief.

'Are we nearly there?' Jenny said again.

They had turned left and were reading the names on the occasional houses they passed.

A dog in the nearby farmhouse barked furiously. The seagulls wheeled over the house, crying to each other.

'Oh, it's lovely,' the mother said. 'Can't you smell the sea?' The sun poured down on a white-painted cottage, on pink fuchsia bushes, red geraniums, and blue hydrangeas.

They got out of the car and rushed round to the back. 'They said the key would be on a hook by the rainwater tank. Yes, here it is.'

She opened the door. Standing facing them was a child's blackboard. On it someone had written:

'WELLCOME TO OUR HOUSE.'

The arrangement had been made back in the winter in letters between parents. Luke and Brenda Simpson had been wondering, as they wondered each winter, where they should go for a holiday. Apart from the money side of it, hotels and guesthouses aren't much fun with a three-year-old, particularly one like Jenny, who was likely to stand up on her chair and demand Rice Krispies in the middle of lunch. She never could tell which meal was which. Actually this seemed quite sensible to Anna – a lot more sensible than some of Jenny's goings-on. Anna herself never could see why certain foods were supposed to belong to certain times. Why shouldn't you have marmalade for tea, or chocolate mousse for breakfast if you wanted to? She would when she was grown up; that was certain.

Anna was nine, and just recently being grown up had begun to seem quite possibly near. She often thought with pleasure of the things she would do when she was grown up, of the long white socks and pretty dresses she would always let her daughters wear, and of the house she would have, as neat and tidy as the ones you see in television commercials.

Stephen was different. He wanted to stay just the way he was. At eleven, he had just left his junior school and was going on in September to a big comprehensive. He had not said much to anyone, least of all to Anna, but he rather wished time would just stand still and hold him for ever in these summer holidays, leaving homework and house captains and all the mysteries of a big strange school still unexplained.

These holidays were especially important to Stephen. He had suggested a camping holiday, but his father wasn't keen on that. He said it was mad to camp in England, and even on the continent it knew if he was sleeping in a tent and rained specially.

Then the letter had come. The mother had picked it up off the mat and looked curiously at the postmark. 'Jersey,' she said. 'I don't know anyone in Jersey.'

'For Sunny Summer Holidays – Jersey.' Anna read out. It was stamped on the letter. 'Perhaps you've won a holiday in Jersey, Mummy.'

'But I've not been in for a competition.'

'Oh, open it,' Stephen said.

His mother opened the Jersey letter and read it quickly. Then she sat down and poured a cup of tea.

'Remember Chris Fisher who was at Bristol with me?' she said.

'No,' said Stephen and Anna.

'Yes, of course,' said their father. 'He got married and went off to America, didn't he?'

'That's right. And now he lives in Jersey. He remembers our house from when he used to come out before he was married – ten or eleven years ago, it must have been. He always liked it and now he's wondering whether we'd enjoy swapping houses for a few weeks in the summer. He misses London.'

'I should think he does,' the father said. 'Imagine living the whole year in a place that size with nothing but Jersey cows and tomatoes and potatoes. What's he doing there?'

'Writing,' the mother said. 'He writes thrillers and it's better for the tax, apparently.'

'It's nice for us, anyway. A holiday in Jersey with only the fares to pay.'

'Hurray,' said Stephen. 'Jersey!'

'I've got a jersey,' Jenny said. 'And some shoes.'

'It's a place,' Anna explained patiently. Then she turned to her father. 'Where is it exactly?'

'There's a group of islands in the Channel; much nearer France than England. It'll be a good swap.'

'What's a swap?' Jenny asked.

'Like swapping stamps,' Stephen said. 'If someone has something you want and you have something he wants, you swap.'

Jenny didn't seem to understand. She was chewing her hair.

'Stop chewing your hair,' her mother said. 'You've just had breakfast.'

'Can I pack then?' Jenny asked. 'Pack my jersey?'

'We're not going till the summer, silly,' Stephen said, tearing the Jersey stamp off the letter to add to his collection.

But at last the summer came and school was over, and their suitcases bulged with clean clothes and treasured objects.

They left their car at London Airport and the key in an envelope for the Fishers to collect at the Enquiry Desk. The two planes, the one with the Fishers going one way, the second with the Simpsons going the other, passed in mid-air, somewhere over the Channel.

Stephen had hoped to see it but there was nothing but cloud. Anna wasn't looking. She was reading her book, which was an exciting one about some children in Scotland who found a treasure in a cave.

When they reached Jersey the sun had come out. They collected the Fishers' car keys from the place marked INFORMATION and found the car waiting for them in the car park. And eventually, after that long winding country drive (Stephen thought they must have been going round in circles for it to take so long), they had reached *La Falaise*.

It was basically an old cottage which had had some bits added on to make it larger and more comfortable. On one side it faced the road and there was a view across fields, with the farmhouse that owned the fields a little farther along on that side of the road. The front garden of *La Falaise* was crammed with flowers. Bees hovered in the lavender. At the side there was a sandy drive leading to a shed which served as a garage.

'WELLCOME TO OUR HOUSE.' Anna read it aloud. 'The girl must have done it. Victoria, didn't you say her name was, Mummy?'

'Yes. She's nine, so her father said, like you, and the little boy, Simon, is six.'

'Six is big,' Jenny said.

The children explored the cottage then, while Luke Simpson brought in the luggage from the car and his wife put on the kettle for a cup of tea. 'You deserve it, Luke. You did very well to get us here in one piece.'

'Five pieces,' he said. 'Not to mention the luggage. How do we have so much stuff?'

He took the cases upstairs and found the children quarrelling about which rooms they should have. They both wanted the back bedroom.

'I got it first, Dad, really I did. I just came in here straightaway and said I'll have this one. This will suit me fine.' Stephen was looking out of the window. The garden ended in a low wall. Beyond the wall the ground dropped away as a steep, tussocky hillside which ran down to the cliffs overhanging the sea. Out at sea, perched on rocks and guarding the coast, there stood a lighthouse. 'This is my room,' Stephen said again.

'No, it's mine. Can't you see? Don't be stupid,' Anna said, waving her hand at the pretty brass bedstead with its patchwork quilt. She loved the room. It was just the sort of room she had always wanted.

'I'm afraid she's right,' their father said. 'Look, Stephen – not out the window but in the room. It's obviously Victoria's room and meant for Anna and Jenny.' Victoria's dolls were sitting along the top of the chest of drawers. And Simon's old cot had been brought out of storage and put up in the corner. In the wardrobe the dresses Victoria hadn't taken to London with her were pushed to one end, and there were spare hangers waiting for Anna and Jenny.

Luke Simpson settled the argument by opening the girls' suitcase and asking Anna to unpack.

'This is your room, Stephen,' he called from the

front. 'You can see the cows in the farm opposite.'

But cows were a poor substitute for the sea and a lighthouse. Stephen started to pull the things out of his suitcase, grumbling.

'Oh, kids,' Luke Simpson said in disgust, going downstairs to the kitchen to collect his cup of tea. 'Never satisfied. We bring them to this lovely place and all they can do is grumble.' He sat down and sipped at the hot tea.

Next moment there was a horrible scream from the garden.

'Jenny!'

They rushed out. The parents from the kitchen, Stephen and Anna jumping down the stairs. There was no sign of her. Then they heard her sobs from beyond the garden wall.

'She's fallen into the sea!' Anna gasped.

Of course, Jenny hadn't. The sea wasn't as near as that. Climbing on to the top of the wall with the help of an apple tree, Jenny had overbalanced and fallen on to the soft turf on the far side. She was more shocked than hurt.

Stephen climbed over to help her back.

Their mother said: 'How can we stop her doing that again? Why weren't you watching her, Anna?'

'I can't watch her *all* the time,' Anna said, in an aggrieved voice. She loved Jenny but there were times when she wished she didn't have a small sister.

'Can I go down to the sea?' Stephen was anxious to explore, but he wasn't allowed to. There was the unpacking to finish and then it would be teatime.

When they were all sitting down to tea, with fresh bread, cold beef, and rasberry icecream which the Fishers had left ready for them, the mother opened the long envelope which had been propped up on the dresser.

Inside there were some sheets of typing paper, held together with a paper clip.

'Good heavens! Do we really need to know all this?

There's a whole page about how to wind the grand-father clock. . . .' Her eye ran down the page. 'Oh, that's all right – he says "Forget it if scared but quite simple".'

The children looked with interest at the wad of paper. 'What else does he say?'

The mother read out some random samples. ' "Knob of bolt on back door falls out. If lost, nail or match-stick will serve. . . . In heavy rain roof likely to leak. You cd collect laddr fm garage and go up into attic to empty and rearrange buckets, or just mop. . . . If in attic you may see birds. Sparrows were around last week. Don't worry. If they got in, they can presum-ably get out, if they want".'

'May we go and see?' Anna asked.

'Not now. Get on with your tea. And listen to this. "Floor in sitting room cd possibly collapse if sub-jected to elephantine stompg. Piano v. good for Lizst." So no elephantine stomping.'

'What's elephantine stomping?' Jenny asked.

'Oh, dancing like an elephant,' Stephen said. 'Go on, Ma.'

'Well, there's more about clocks. One of them needs "magic incantations" apparently. And the "cup-board under stairs will open with slight bash at lower right hand corner". Then there's lots about shops and bakers and newspapers and milk, and the best beaches and putting the dustbins out each Monday "where front gate wd be if there ws one".'

'Did you write all that sort of stuff out for them?' Stephen wanted to know.

'No I didn't, really. Just a few notes here and there. "Window-cleaner calls second Tuesday" and that sort of thing. I wonder how they'll manage.'

Anna was reading the typescript, holding it in one hand and a bit of bread and butter in the other. When she got to the last page, she exclaimed 'Oh look, Victoria must have added this at the end. It says "WATCH OUT FOR THE ONLY TREASURE".'

TWO

The Battle of Flowers

Anna was excited. What could Victoria mean? How was she to watch out for the treasure? Were there to be no clues? Of course, if Victoria had known where the treasure was she would have found it herself by now. Presumably she didn't know anything except that there was one. Anna wasn't really surprised. Treasure was always cropping up in the books she read. There usually seemed to be some hidden sovereigns or doubloons knocking about when people went on holiday.

And where was treasure normally found? In attics or in caves. There wasn't much point in searching the Fishers' attic. She might just poke around a bit when she went up to see if the sparrows were still there. But Victoria would obviously have done that herself. Caves were another matter. The children in the book she was reading at the moment were hunting for treasure in Scottish caves. And there would be so many in a place like Jersey.

Anna's thoughts were interrupted by Jenny saying 'Carry me! Carry me!' They had come out for a walk after tea. Jenny should really have been in bed but everyone wanted to go down to the sea, and it wouldn't matter for once if Jenny had a late night.

Stephen and his father were ahead but waiting for the others to catch up. Jenny climbed up on Anna's back. They were going down to the sea, not by the shortest possible route beyond the garden wall: that was too steep. And not by the road, which looped and wandered half way round the island, it seemed, before coming to rest in the fishing village below them. Instead they walked down the edge of a tomato field. The earth was like dust for there had been no rain for some time. The plants leaned against their stakes in neat rows, heavy with their fruit.

'I'd forgotten the smell of growing tomatoes,' the mother said.

'Mm,' said Anna, sniffing. 'Quite different from shop ones.'

Stephen and his father had taken two stakes from a pile in one corner of the field and were having a mock sword fight.

'Can I have this one?' Jenny asked, when they reached them. She had slipped off Anna's back and was holding up a broken stake. 'It's a little one for me.'

'No,' said Anna positively. 'They might need it for a newborn tomato plant.'

'And you might stick it in your eye,' her mother said.

They came out of the field by a gate on to the road just above the first small cottages of the village, which huddled together with their backs to the hillside. The road became a village street, cobbled and lined with pubs and shops. At the end they could see the sea and smell it in their nostrils.

Then they came out on to the seafront, like emerging from a tunnel into a wide open space. There was a little harbour, full of boats, protected by a breakwater, a small beach littered with seaweed, rocks, and rockpools to the west, and out to sea the tall white shape of the lighthouse they had seen from Victoria's bedroom window.

Fishermen's nets draped the harbour wall. To the right, there was the terrace of an expensive-looking hotel. 'Fleuron Bay Hotel,' Anna read. Smart people sat around on the terrace drinking drinks, and at one table Anna noticed a girl of about her own age sitting by herself. She was very pretty, with long fair hair. It was beautifully smooth, as if she brushed it a hundred times night and morning. It was held back from her face by a dark blue hairband. Her dress was the same colour. It looked new.

Anna glanced down at her own cotton frock, crumpled from the plane journey, dirtied by Jenny's sandals. She sighed. She hated to be shabby. If only she could look like the hotel girl. Stephen's hair was as fair but Anna's own was that in-between colour usually called mousy, though most mice are grey.

The hotel girl was perfect in every detail from the top of her shining fair head to her long white socks and

black patent-leather shoes. She sat at the table, sipping an orange drink from a tall glass full of ice and slices of orange.

Stephen and Jenny and their parents had jumped down on to the beach and were turning over bits and pieces: smooth pebbles and shells and bits of drift-wood. They had all taken their shoes off except Stephen. Anna heard her mother call out, 'There's some tar, Stephen. Take your shoes off. Feet wash more easily than shoes.'

'Yes,' said Stephen. 'But we've got several pairs of shoes and only one pair of feet.' He really didn't care about his shoes or his feet. But now he took off his shoes to be obliging and splashed about in the wet sand at the water's edge. Specks of sand flew up and spattered his clothes. 'Come on, Anna,' he called. 'What are you doing?' Jenny had found a lobster's claw and was scratching her leg with it.

Anna gave a last admiring look at the shining hotel girl and started to undo her sandals. She left them on the wall and jumped down on to the beach. She was so grubby already, it couldn't make much difference. But if she found that treasure, she would have new white socks every day. Twice a day sometimes. And she would stay at a hotel with a terrace and not in a cottage which would fall to pieces if an elephant called in for a dance.

She sighed. How could you find a treasure without clues?

Anna woke next morning to hear the rain. 'Just our bad luck,' she thought, 'when they haven't had any rain for weeks.' She looked up to see if there was any rain coming through the roof yet. It looked a bit stained but not actually wet. The buckets must be doing their work. Jenny was still asleep, lying on her back in the cot completely uncovered. Anna went across and pulled a blanket over her. Then she picked up her book from the bedside table and started reading. When she got to the end of the chapter she paused. She wished there was a map. It was rather confusing, but it seemed the children had found the right cave at last; it was just a question of getting into it. They were lucky. There had been clues, of course: a sixty-year-old letter mentioning old fishermen and the cave on the south side, a phrase that had been handed down about finding Esau's cave and getting rich.

But where could *she* start? She could write to Victoria, of course, in London and ask her if she knew any more. But no, if she had she would have said. Anna would simply have to do what Victoria had suggested and 'watch out'.

She looked out at the rain again. It would be difficult to do anything if this went on. Then she realized that the rain was even worse than it had at first appeared. Today was the day of the Battle of Flowers in St Helier and their parents had promised to take them. ('If I can get the car into gear,' Luke Simpson had said. But she was sure he would.) If only the rain would stop.

It was still raining after breakfast. Stephen and his father were playing Scrabble rather loudly, and Jenny was dancing to a record. 'Just as well she's not an elephant,' Anna thought, looking at the floor with some anxiety. It was covered with a carpet but she couldn't help wondering what was going on underneath. There was too much noise for her to read. The Wally Whyton record seemed to fill the whole house. She was gazing out of the window at the rain when she noticed the summerhouse at the end of the garden, beyond the apple tree.

'"Jersey for sunny summer holidays"' her mother said behind her.

'Can I go out to the summerhouse for some peace-and-quiet, Ma?' Her mother was always begging for a little peace-and-quiet herself, so Anna thought she would be sympathetic.

'Yes. Wait a minute. There's a key here somewhere. I'm sure it will be all right if you just want to read. Don't touch anything.' She gave Anna a key with a label on saying – STUDY – 'This must be it. There's nowhere else it could be.'

Anna slipped on her raincoat, holding her book under it to keep it dry. Rain dripped on her head off the summerhouse roof as she struggled to turn the key.

There was a mat inside the door and she wiped her feet carefully and hung up her coat behind the door. She remembered that her mother had said Christopher Fisher was a writer. This must be where he did all his work. She looked round with interest. She had never been in a writer's study before.

It was a small room. There were book shelves up to the ceiling on one wall and below them a wider shelf topped with black formica running from wall to wall. This was obviously used as a desk. There was a type-writer at one end with a box of typing paper beside it on one side, and on the other a mug with three or four pipes in it, a box of matches and an ashtray. Anna could just imagine this man she had never seen, tipping his chair back and sucking a pipe as he tried to think of the next bit to write. She sat in the chair to see what it felt like, and wished she could type. 'QWERTY UIOP', she read off the top row of letters. Whoever decided to put them in that order? Wouldn't it be much simpler to follow the alphabet?

On the bookshelf immediately above the desk there was a row of books, some in English and some in other languages, all with the name *Christopher Fisher* on the spine. Anna was very impressed. She wanted to take one down but remembered her mother's words: 'Don't touch anything.'

She settled down in the armchair in one corner with *Strangers at the Door*. It was exciting. The children had managed to find the right cave in Chapter Nine. Well, they thought it was the right one. But they hadn't got a torch with them. How stupid of them not to think of that. She must remember herself. There was that little one she had had in her stocking at Christmas, but the battery had run out from reading under the bedclothes and she hadn't brought it to Jersey. She must see if the Fishers had one anywhere.

She got up to go and have a look and realized she had been sitting in an awkward position in the armchair. The foot that had been tucked under her was full of pins and needles. She could see why they were called pins and needles. It was as if hundreds of goblins were sticking tiny pins and needles into her. She hopped around the room to try and get rid of them, and noticed something she had not noticed before. The wall to her left was covered in cork tiles and lots of different things were pinned upon it. In the middle there was a huge map of Jersey. There were some postcards and bits cut from newspapers and a piece of typing paper with the words WORK SCHEDULE at the top and lots of dates and numbers underneath. Anna supposed that if you didn't have to be at work each day as most people did you had to plan what you did at home, or days might pass in just doing things like watering the tomatoes and painting the kitchen.

Then something else caught Anna's eye. Pinned rather high up (she had to stand on the desk chair to examine it properly) there was a map drawn in blue felt-pen. It was a map of the area round the cottage – there were the words *La Falaise* in neat letters, then *Fleuron Bay* and the road going down to it. There were other lines, too, which obviously indicated roads they had not yet explored, and there were three crosses in red. One was a short way along the coast from Fleuron Bay, the others were both much nearer the cottages, probably only a few minutes walk away in different directions. Anna wondered what it was all about. Then, of course, she knew. These were the clues she was looking for. A map was even better than an old letter. She remembered the one she'd seen in the copy of *Treasure Island* Stephen had been reading a month or two before.

Forgetting conveniently what her mother had said about not touching anything, Anna took a clean sheet of typewriting paper from the box on Christopher Fisher's desk, found a ball-pen sticking out of the mug with the pipes, and began to copy the map as carefully as she could.

She had nearly finished when Stephen came rushing in. 'It's stopped raining, you idiot. Didn't you notice? The sun's come out. What are you doing?'

Anna had jumped down and shoved the map into her book with an instinct for secrecy. Later she would transfer it to her purse.

'Just reading,' she said.

'Standing up on a chair?' He glanced at the big map on the wall, not noticing the small hand-drawn one. 'Oh, that's the same as the one in the car. Dad's been studying it for this afternoon. You know we're going down to St Helier, for the Battle of the Flowers.'

'What do they do?' Anna asked. She had meant to ask before.

'Throw flowers at each other, I should think,' Stephen said. 'Mum says would we pick some tomatoes for lunch.'

The car wouldn't start. Well, it did start in the ordinary sense. The engine purred into life when Luke Simpson turned the ignition key. It didn't even need the choke. But however much he tried to get into first gear (consulting the diagram in the handbook every few minutes) he just didn't seem able to manage it. When he thought it was in, the car shot backwards in reverse and nearly knocked down the back wall of the garage. He put his foot on the brake just in time.

'It's ridiculous,' the father said for the fourth time. Everyone was sitting in the car, clean and tidy for the trip to St Helier, trying not to make any irritating remarks.

Then the mother suggested, 'I could go into the shop and see if anyone could help. Someone might know the Renault's peculiarities.' There was a store just along the road.

'All right,' the father said grudgingly. He hated to appear such a fool.

They all got out of the car. Anna and Stephen took Jenny across to look at the calf tethered in the field opposite. He was a small brown calf with a white splash on his forehead and a stripe across his back. 'Wouldn't it be odd if we had striped hair,' Stephen said. 'It would make it more interesting really.'

They noticed some children watching them from the wall of the farmyard. There were two of them, a boy and a girl, grubby and brown in boots and jeans. They seemed to be smiling.

'I bet they're laughing at Dad for not being able to start the car,' Stephen said.

'Beasts,' Anna said. She turned her back on them deliberately.

The mother went into the shop down the road. There was a woman behind the counter, slicing bacon and humming to herself. 'Oh, hullo, Mrs Simpson,' she said, recognizing her, for she had been in after breakfast with a long shopping list. 'Forgotten something, did you? How about a little of this nice streaky?'

'No, thank you. Not today. I'm afraid I've come in about the Fishers' car. It got us here yesterday, but now we can't get it started and we want to go down to St Helier for the Battle of the Flowers.'

The shopkeeper glanced at her watch. 'Oh dear, you'll miss it at this rate,' she said. 'Just a minute.'

She went out the back and returned with her husband. 'Philip will see what he can do. He knows the Renault. His Papa has one the same.'

Philip was a man of few words, but he soon showed Luke the knack of engaging first gear. The children waved to him as the car sailed off down the road.

Jenny said, 'I love that man.'

When they got to St Helier, it seemed quite deserted. There were cars parked everywhere and they had some difficulty in finding a place. But, apart from the cars, the streets were quite empty.

They walked downhill, confident that this would lead them to the seafront where the Battle of Flowers was being held.

There were red posters everywhere. Most of them seemed to be in French.

LA PREMIÈRE FÊTE DES FLEURS
D'EUROPE

Their father translated one for them. 'It says there are fifty floats decorated entirely with flowers.'

'What are floats?' Anna asked. 'Are they on the sea?'

'No, they just go along the road. They can be anything really – lorries or trailers, normally. There just has to be space on them to create a scene in flowers and for people to sit.'

'Are we nearly there?' Jenny was asking. They had brought Simon Fisher's old pushchair which they had found conveniently hanging up on a nail in the garage, but Jenny refused to ride in it.

They were getting near the seafront – they could hear a band in the distance and smell the sea – when suddenly the street was full of people coming, as it were, to meet them.

After the morning's rain, the sky was clear and blue and the people streaming towards them were in shirt sleeves and summer dresses. Lots of them were licking icecreams or eating crisps out of bags. They had the purposeless look of people on holiday with nothing particular to do. They peered in shop windows and straggled across the road, eager to go on enjoying themselves but uncertain what to do before teatime.

'It must be over,' Luke Simpson said.

'Oh *no*, Dad,' Stephen said.

'It's not fair,' said Anna.

'Are we nearly there?' Jenny asked again.

They decided to go on, though it was difficult, like swimming against the tide, with everyone else going in the opposite direction.

They came out on to the seafront and Stephen climbed up on top of the seawall to see if he could find out if there was anything still going on. 'I can see some of the floats,' he said.

A helicopter passed over them dropping showers of coloured paper on the crowd.

'It should be petals,' Anna said. 'Come on, Stephen.' They pushed through the crowd in the direction of the floats. There was a barrier across the road with ticket offices, but no one was taking any money now it was all over, and Stephen and Anna were able to pass through.

Jenny was busy picking up pieces of coloured tissue paper from the ground. 'One, two, four, six.' She clutched them in her small hand.

'Oh come on, darling,' her mother said. 'We'll lose the others.'

A man with long hair and a funny hat had jumped up on the seawall and was strumming a guitar. There was a long queue at an icecream van. The road was lined with cafés and travel agents and shops selling films and cigarettes and big peaches for a shilling each.

When they got beyond the ticket barriers, the crowds had thinned out quite a lot, but they could see no sign of Stephen or Anna.

Policemen in white sun helmets stood in the middle of the road and kept the way clear for the floats to find their way home now that the parade was over.

Farther along the front, Stephen and Anna had a

marvellous view. They stood on the kerb and watched the floats trundle past.

'I'm glad we were late,' Anna said. 'Look, there's Dr Dolittle.' There was an enormous model of the great sea snail all covered in pink flowers. 'And that's the Olympic Games.' There were scenes made of flowers which were supposed to be in Mexico, and athletic-looking girls and men were pulling the float. Then there was a model of a vintage car, there was a huge crossword puzzle, there was a map of Jersey, there were Jersey cows and there was a scene showing the making of cider. And everything they could see was made of flowers.

'It's not exactly a battle, is it?' Anna said.

'No, but perhaps I can pull a flower off and throw it at you,' Stephen said, grabbing a hydrangea from the float that was passing. But a voice called out to him to leave it alone. Stephen looked confused and stuffed it in his pocket.

'This is a lovely one,' Anna said. 'I like this one best.'

The last float of all had a fairy-tale castle on one end, its towers of white dahlias with the roofs in red. At the other end there was a little cottage, all made of flowers and covered in climbing roses. In between the two were models of the seven dwarfs, made entirely of flowers. There was just one living person on the float – Snow White.

She sat on a small red chair with her hands folded in

her lap. She had a dark blue dress down to her ankles and her long fair hair was held back by a hair band of the same colour.

Suddenly Anna recognized her. 'It's the hotel girl,' she said, 'the girl from Fleuron Bay. Oh, isn't she beautiful.' Anna waved at her as she went past but she sat as still as a statue.

At that moment, Stephen felt a hand on his shoulder. He thought for a moment that it was the police arresting him for plucking the flower from the float, but it was only his father.

'Here you are at last,' Luke Simpson said. 'We've been looking for you everywhere. We were just going over to ask them to make an announcement over the loudspeaker.'

'Did you think we were lost?' Stephen said. 'We weren't, you know. We were just standing here waiting for you.'

'Did you see Snow White?' Anna asked. 'It was the girl from the hotel. Isn't she beautiful?'

'I liked the dwarfs better,' Stephen said. 'Do you think there's time for a swim?'

They looked over the seawall. The tide was a long way out and the beach and rocks were littered with the coloured paper from the helicopter. A lot of people had gone down to the beach when they had finished watching the parade and the sand was thick with people, stretched out and cooking themselves in the sun.

'It's really rather horrid,' Anna said. The seafront

had an abandoned look now the last float had gone. A
gust of wind caught some of the ice lolly wrappers and
tissue paper and sent them swirling.

'They're going to have a job clearing this lot up,'
Anna said. She wished everything could be as beautiful
and tidy as Snow White.

Jenny had now agreed to ride in the pushchair. She
was tired and sat there silently, sucking her fingers.

'Let's go back to the cottage and swim at Fleuron
Bay tomorrow,' their father said.

THREE

The hotel girl

They were having breakfast in the cottage when they heard a small noise and the children rushed out to the back garden to find a fluffy ginger kitten chasing his own tail.

Anna was thrilled.

Jenny was not so sure. 'He'll eat me,' she said, trying to hide behind Anna.

'Of course he won't. Let's ask Ma for some milk for him.' But their mother said it wasn't a good idea to put out milk for him. 'If you do, you'll never get rid of him.'

'I don't want to get rid of him,' Anna said. 'He's sweet.'

Stephen said, 'I wonder where he came from.' He picked the kitten up and tucked him inside his shirt.

'Someone will be missing him,' their mother said, beginning to clear the table.

'Oh, I shouldn't worry,' their father said, screwing the top on the marmalade jar. 'It's like the sparrows in the attic. If he got in, he can presumably get out again. Put him on the wall, Stephen.'

Stephen put the kitten on the wall but he jumped back into the garden of *La Falaise*.

'He likes it here,' Stephen said. He stroked the kitten's back. Jenny plucked up courage and came over to stroke the kitten, too, starting at the tail and ruffling up his fur.

'Not that way,' Stephen said. 'Like this, silly.' He guided her hand.

Jenny was very pleased with her courage and danced around in a circle, singing '"Pussy cat, pussy cat, where have you been?"'

'Well, not to London, that's certain,' Anna said. 'He couldn't afford a ticket on the plane.'

Their mother called from the kitchen, 'Oh, leave that kitten alone and come and help with the drying up.' Anna took a tea towel and her mother suddenly noticed what she was wearing.

'You're looking terribly smart this morning, Anna. You can't wear that down to the beach. What on earth did you put it on for?'

Anna dried a plate carefully before she answered. It was difficult to think of a reason that did not sound silly.

'I wanted to look nice,' she said.

'But you look very nice in your blue shorts and that red T-shirt. And it's stupid to risk messing up your good clothes. You might get tar on it or anything.'

The real reason was that Anna hoped to get to know the hotel girl that morning, and she wanted to look her best. She had on her favourite dress, which had small blue roses on it, and her newest white socks. She had brushed her hair for ages before coming down to breakfast, but it wasn't the right sort of hair. It never looked tidy for five minutes.

Anna supposed the girl was staying at the Fleuron Bay Hotel and it might be easy enough to get into conversation with her. She hoped the girl would help look for Victoria's treasure. It would be more fun having someone to help and she didn't want Stephen.

'Go and change, please, Anna,' her mother was saying.

'No, I'm not going to,' Anna said. She put away the cup she was drying, hung up the tea towel tidily and rushed out of the kitchen. 'I'm not going to the beach anyway, and I shan't mess it up.'

Her mother sighed. 'No, I don't suppose you will.'

Anna took care of her clothes. Sometimes her mother felt appearances were the things she really cared about. It had always been the same even when she was a really small child.

Anna ran down the road. She would go the long way down to the Bay to make sure of not dirtying her clothes. When she was out of sight of the house and was sure no one was coming after her, she slowed down and thought about what she was going to do.

She had her purse in the pocket of her dress and she supposed there was nothing to stop her walking up the steps to the terrace, sitting on one of the chairs and asking the waiter for a drink, as if she did it every day.

It was lovely walking down to the village. It was a clear, sunny morning but there had been some rain in the night and everything had been washed clean. The road was high-hedged and the banks below the hedges were studded with wild flowers, growing so neatly and brightly together that it reminded Anna of a patch-work quilt, each patch in a frame of green. Some of the green was ivy and fern, and she picked these, too, with the purple loosestrife, red campion, and scarlet pimpernel, liking the way the green showed up the bright colours. Drops of rain lurked inside some of the flowers.

Anna found she was still clutching them when she walked up the steps of the Fleuron Bay Hotel, and she felt foolish, but it was too late to throw them away.

There were very few people on the terrace as it was still early. There was an elderly man with a bald head, a pot of coffee, and a copy of *The Times*. There were two middle-aged women, both knitting and both smiling quietly at the scene before them, as if they were determined to show they were enjoying their holiday. There was no sign of the girl in the dark blue dress.

Anna sat down at the table nearest the steps. It was the same table the girl had been sitting at. She smoothed her skirt carefully under her and put down the wild flowers tidily in front of her.

A young waiter in a white cotton jacket and black trousers appeared. He smiled at Anna, said 'Allow me' and picked up the little bunch of wild flowers. Without saying anything else, he carried them out through the swingdoors that led to the kitchens.

Anna thought he had gone to throw them away, but in a moment he was back with the wild flowers arranged in a small glass vase. He put it carefully in the middle of Anna's table.

Anna's cheeks felt pink. But she noticed that *The Times* man was still reading his paper and the knitting women were still knitting. She relaxed a little and said 'That's nice. Thank you very much.'

'And what can I do for you?' the waiter said.

'I'd like some orange juice, please, and could you tell me if there's anyone of my age, a girl about my age, staying here for the holidays?'

'No, I'm afraid there's not,' the waiter said. 'It's not really a family hotel, you understand.' He lowered his voice. 'It's expensive, you see, and the residents – they don't like a lot of noise. We have got a couple of boys, as a matter of fact, at the moment but they're big ones. Youths, you'd call them, really. Spend all their time water ski-ing. They're no trouble.'

Anna was very disappointed. The waiter didn't seem in a hurry so she went on, 'I saw this girl, you see, sitting here on the terrace the other night and then I saw her in the Battle of Flowers. She's very beautiful.'

'Oh, of course,' the waiter laughed. 'Silly of me. But you did say "staying here for the holidays". Oh dear me, yes. There's her all right.'

Anna waited for him to go on but as he didn't she prompted him. 'Who is she then?'

'That was our Miss Felicity, that was – the beautiful Miss Felicity Le Brun. And she wasn't staying here. Oh no, she *lives* here. Her Mum and Dad own the place and you can say that again.' He broke off as the glass doors from the main hall of the hotel swung open and Felicity herself came out on to the terrace.

'I'll get your orange juice, miss,' the waiter said rather hurriedly, and went off to the kitchen.

Felicity looked round in rather a bored way. She was obviously wondering what to do with herself and how best to pass the morning.

Her eyes slid over *The Times* man and the knitting women and came to rest on Anna.

Anna's hand went instinctively to her head to smooth down her hair. Felicity came over to the table and said to Anna, 'Mind if I sit here?'

'No, of course not,' Anna said. 'I mean, I couldn't anyway, could I? They're all your tables really, aren't they?'

'Has Fred been talking to you?' Felicity asked. 'He's not supposed to talk to the guests. He's got plenty to do inside.'

Just at this moment Fred appeared with Anna's orange juice and a small folded piece of paper which he tucked under the vase of wild flowers.

'What on earth are these?' Felicity asked.

'Oh, they're mine,' Anna said, and as the waiter went back into the kitchen, she added, 'Fred was very kind and put them in a vase for me, and you mustn't be cross with him for talking to me. It was all my fault. I asked him about you, you see. I'd seen you here the other day, and then I saw you yesterday being Snow White. You were super.'

'The Battle of Flowers is an awful bore, really. We have it every year, you know. It attracts the tourists.'

'Yes, we're tourists and it attracted us,' Anna said. 'We didn't pay, though. We got there late and it was nearly over and we just stood on the edge and watched everything go by. I liked you best.'

'It was a lovely dress,' Felicity said. 'Would you like to see it? It's up in my room.'

'Oh yes, please.' Anna finished the orange juice and

picked up the little bit of paper and unfolded it. 'Two shillings,' she gasped. 'You can just about buy a whole bottle of orange squash for that,' she thought. 'Where do I pay?'

'Oh, don't worry about that,' Felicity said, with a lordly wave of her hand. 'I'll see to that later.'

'Oh, thank you very much. You are kind.'

Some guests had just arrived from the airport, and the hall of the hotel was full of people and suitcases which looked as if they had never been used before.

A thin woman with dark red hair and a very white skin was greeting the guests. She broke off for a minute when Felicity and Anna came in and started to edge their way through the throng. 'Have you found a little friend, darling one?' she purred. 'So nice for you.'

Anna didn't like being called little, but she was glad Felicity's mother (for so she rightly assumed it was) approved of her. She followed Felicity up the sweeping staircase and along a corridor to the right. Felicity pushed open a door marked PRIVATE and they went in. The room was full of poodles. For a second, Anna thought they were real but then she realized they were just toy ones. They were of all sizes and of all colours, but mostly white, and many of them had bright ribbons round their necks.

Felicity picked up a little black one with a scarlet ribbon. She started brushing it idly. 'I collect them,' she said. 'This is Pipette. What's your name?'

'Anna Simpson,' Anna said. What a plain name it

sounded. She wished she was called Francesca or Jeanette. She went over to the window.

'What a lovely view. You are lucky, Felicity.' There was a window seat, and sitting on it she could see Fleuron Bay spread out before her – the jetty to the left, the little harbour full of brightly coloured boats.

'I used to have a room at the back. It was so dark, right under the hillside with nothing to see but trees. Mama and Papa really wanted this one for the guests, but I made such a fuss they gave it to me last year. I find I can usually get my own way if I make enough fuss, don't you?'

Anna gulped. She didn't think anyone had asked her such a question before. 'Yes, I suppose so. But I don't like rows much.'

'Oh no, neither do I,' Felicity said, putting Pipette aside and taking down a larger white poodle. 'Rows are terribly boring. We can't have them here, anyway, because of the guests. I never have to go as far as a row. They'll give me anything to keep me quiet.' She lay back on her bed and stretched.

Anna had picked up Pipette. The red ribbon round its neck had come undone and she tied it in a big bow.

'You can have Pipette, if you like,' Felicity said.

Anna started to say thank you, but Felicity interrupted. 'Oh, I said I'd show you my Snow White dress. It's in the wardrobe.' She got it out and spread it on the bed. 'I usually wear blue. It matches my eyes.'

46

'It's really lovely,' Anna said. 'Why don't you put it on? I'd love to see you in it again.'

Felicity slipped off the dress she was wearing and pulled the Snow White one over her head. There was a large mirror almost covering one wall of the room and Felicity paraded in front of it like a model girl.

'Would you like to be a model? I'd love to be but my hair's all wrong and I'm sure I shan't be tall enough,' Anna sighed.

'I think it would be rather boring,' Felicity said.

47

'All that walking up and down.' She got a box of chocolate kittens out of her drawer and offered one to Anna. 'I'd rather be an air hostess, flying all round the world. My French would be useful and Papa knows lots of people in BEA.' She took off the dress again and hung it up in the wardrobe.

Anna licked the chocolate kitten slowly. It was so pretty she couldn't bear it to disappear. 'I wanted to ask you something,' she said between licks. 'Are there any caves just along the coast here?'

'Yes, lots. Why?'

'I'm on the track of some treasure,' Anna said importantly.

'Treasure?'

'Yes. Victoria Fisher, that's the girl whose house we're in, left me a message about it.'

'Victoria Fisher? I know her and Simon. You're staying at *La Falaise*, are you? They're just a couple of silly kids. It will be some kids' game.'

'No,' Anna said. 'You see, there's a map their father did, with red crosses marking the possible places, and it was in his study. He wouldn't have drawn the map if it was just a game.'

Felicity began to look interested. 'Tell me more about it.'

Anna pulled her copy of the map out of her purse. She'd had to fold it up very small to fit it in and she smoothed out the creases as best she could before showing it to Felicity.

48

'I'm not sure about these ones,' Felicity said, pointing to the inland crosses. 'They could be any number of places up near *La Falaise*. But I know this cave.' She pointed to the red cross on the coast.

'Could we go this afternoon?' Anna asked.

'No, not today. I'm going surfriding at St Ouen's Bay, with my friend, Suzanne Renouf. Her parents have the Norman Hotel there. There's no hurry, anyway, is there? If the treasure's been there hundreds of years, another day won't matter. Come tomorrow, if you like. It has to be low tide. We'll check at the desk. Come down at about ten, that should be about right, judging by today.' She looked out of the window.

Anna looked too, and to her astonishment saw, at that moment, her parents, Stephen and Jenny walking in the road below, laden with bathing things, folding chairs, rubber balls, the inflatable raft, baskets. And yet it was not so amazing. They had said they were going to swim at Fleuron Bay that morning.

'Must you join them?' Felicity asked, when Anna explained the position.

'I think I should,' Anna said. 'But I promised I wouldn't go on the beach in this dress.'

Felicity raised her eyebrows a little, then she went over to the wardrobe and pulled a blue and white striped shift off its hanger.

'Have this,' she said. 'It's dreadfully old and I never wear it.'

'It doesn't look old,' Anna said.

49

'Oh, go on,' Felicity said impatiently. 'You can bring it back tomorrow, if you want to.'

Anna ran along the beach in the blue and white shift. She carried her dress with the blue roses carefully over one arm, and Pipette the toy poodle was tucked under the other. Remembering what her mother had said about feet being more easily washed than shoes, she had her sandals in one hand. She could see her parents putting up their chairs at the far end of the beach with the rocks behind them. Stephen was pumping up the raft. Jenny was already digging in the sand.

'I've got the most wonderful friend,' she gasped, out of breath with her running. She flopped down on the sand beside her mother. 'She lent me this dress so I could come down on the beach and she showed me the one she wore as Snow White, and her parents run the hotel, and I didn't have to pay for my orange juice. And her name's Felicity and she's given me this poodle.'

'Want the poodle,' Jenny said. She had abandoned her bucket and spade to listen to Anna.

'Well, you can't have it.' Then she saw Jenny was going to cry and relented a little. 'But I'll lend it to you sometimes.'

FOUR

A summons to obey

On the way back to *La Falaise* for lunch, trudging up the steep hillside beside the tomato field with Jenny on her father's back, they passed the children from the farm. These were the children who had seemed to be laughing at Luke Simpson the day before when he'd been unable to get the car moving. They were still wearing their jeans and boots.

They had tied a rope to one of the trees at the edge of the tomato field and were using it as a sort of swing. They grinned at the Simpsons as they passed and Luke Simpson said, 'Good morning' to them.

'I wish I could have a go on that rope,' Stephen said enviously, when they were out of earshot. He was laden with beach gear.

'I don't,' Anna said. 'They look horrid.'

Her mother raised her eyebrows. 'Why horrid, Anna?'

'Oh, rough, you know. Their jeans were all muddy. I didn't like the look of them.'

Luke Simpson passed his family, pretending to be a horse for Jenny. He overheard Anna and slowed his gallop to say 'Appearances can be deceptive, like the wolf in sheep's clothing. It works the other way too.'

Anna looked puzzled, not quite sure what he was talking about.

They reached *La Falaise* a few minutes later. The ginger kitten was lying in the sun in the garden. When he heard them he stretched and came over to rub himself against Anna's legs.

'It doesn't want to go home, Mummy. I'm sure we should give him some lunch.'

'I wonder where he lives,' Stephen said.

'Pussy cat, pussy cat, where have you been?' Jenny asked.

'He'll soon go home when he's hungry,' their mother assured them.

'I'm hungry, anyway,' Stephen said. 'Ravenous. Voracious.' Those were good words. He said them again, several times.

'Well, put those things away – Anna, you hang up the swimming things on the line – and then come and help me get lunch.' Anna and Stephen groaned but went to do as they were told.

They were sitting at lunch in the kitchen when they heard a small noise in the garden. It was a sort of thud.

'Well, that's not the kitten,' Stephen said.

'Can we go and see?' Anna asked, not waiting for an answer.

'Why is it never possible for those children to sit

at the table for a whole meal,' their father wondered. 'Always jumping up in the middle. I'm sure it's bad for their digestions.'

'It doesn't seem to be,' their mother said honestly. 'They've never had indigestion in their lives.'

Out in the garden, Stephen and Anna found the kitten had gone and in its place, sitting in the middle of the lawn, was a strange parcel.

A large piece of paper, which looked as if it had been torn from a school exercise book, had been wrapped round a stone and tied at the top with a piece of thin string.

'What's it for?' Anna asked, picking up the stone and examining it. 'It's just an ordinary pebble.'

'Oh, that's just a weight,' Stephen said. 'It's this that counts.' He spread the piece of paper out on the grass. On it someone had written:

TO THE BOY WITH FAIR HAIR —

COME TO THE EMPTY HOUSE BY

THE MILL AT 2.30 TODAY OR ELSE.

TOP SECRET.

Anna felt cold inside although the sun was still shining.

'What's it about, Stephen? You'd better ask Daddy.'

'No. I'll find out for myself.'

'I wish Felicity were here.'

'Oh, Felicity. I'm sick of hearing about how wonderful she is.' Anna had talked about her half the morning and all through lunch.

'Well, I'll come with you,' Anna said. It was the last thing she wanted to do, and she couldn't help being glad when Stephen said: 'No, you're not coming, and I'm not telling anyone about it and you're not to either.' He put the piece of paper in his pocket and tossed the pebble on to the flowerbed.

'We don't want it getting in the lawn mower when the grass is cut,' he said in a matter-of-fact voice, as if he was in the habit of getting mysterious notes every day of the week.

'It might have had finger prints on it,' Anna said, looking at the stone where it had fallen by a clump of yellow dahlias. 'Where's the empty house, anyway? I haven't seen one.'

'At least we know where the windmill is. It's just round the bend in the road from the shop. I noticed it yesterday.'

'Oh, I know,' Anna said. 'It hasn't got any arms.'

'Sails,' Stephen said.

'Children!' Their mother was calling from the kitchen. 'Come and finish your lunch.'

Stephen put his pullover on before slipping out of *La Falaise* at a quarter past two. He wanted to be in plenty of time. It was still a warm day but he felt he needed some protection. Not that a pullover was a suit of armour, but it seemed to help a bit. He had given

Anna the impression that he wasn't worried but inside himself he was a little frightened. He had read things in the papers and had heard about big boys who beat people up for their own amusement. Well, if anything nasty happened to him, at least Anna knew where he was. He rather wished he had let her come with him. It would feel better not to be alone.

In fact, he was *not* alone. Anna was following him. She didn't want to do it but in the end had known she had to find out what Stephen had let himself in for. After lunch she had gone up to her room and taken off Felicity's blue and white shift and put on her shorts and red T-shirt. Then she sat by the window of her parent's bedroom, reading *Strangers at the Door* with one eye and watching the front drive with the other.

Somehow, now that things were happening in real life, the book didn't seem quite as exciting as it had before. She found it difficult to concentrate on those adventures in Scotland. She was glad when she saw Stephen come quietly round the corner of the house and turn left. It was easier to be doing something.

It was simple enough to follow Stephen without being seen, for he never looked back. Anna had to keep a good way behind him in case he sensed that he was being followed, and she walked silently on the grass at the roadside. Stephen's own footsteps thudded regularly on the tarmac and Anna felt her own heart was beating in time with them and as loudly. But he didn't hear. She had one disturbing moment when he stopped suddenly and she thought he was going to turn round, but he just bent down to tie the lace on his shoe and went on without hesitation.

The mill was tall and solid, built of local stone. It stood where the road they were in joined another, smaller road, a lane really, with high hedges, which ran inland and uphill. There was a notice at the corner saying NO THROUGH ROAD.

Stephen turned the corner and walked up the lane. It was completely deserted. Anna realized how little used it must be, for grass grew down the middle of the lane. In a few minutes it twisted and a drive ran up from the lefthand side to a drab cottage. Its garden was overgrown, the drive itself almost choked with nettles except for a narrow track which ran up the middle.

Anna could see that there were no curtains at the windows of the cottage and, indeed, that one of them was broken. This was certainly the place.

She dropped down into the long grass at the roadside as Stephen started to walk, slowly but firmly, up the track, careful not to sting himself. She could still see him as he came to the top of the slope and out into the open space in front of the cottage.

The slight exertion of climbing uphill must have made him feel too hot, and he crossed his arms, gripped the bottom of his pullover and started to take it off. He must have been unable to see for just five seconds and in that five seconds Anna, watching in the long grass, saw two boys rush out and grab him. Stephen cried out and Anna sprang up and started to go to his help. But she knew almost at once that it was no use. She was no match for the boys. They had been so busy with their prisoner that they hadn't noticed Anna and she sank back into the long grass, unobserved, to see what would happen next. One of the boys held in his hands a scarf—a coloured cotton one. Anna thought even in that moment of fear that he must have taken it from his mother's drawer.

The two boys held the struggling Stephen and tied the scarf round his eyes. Then a third boy appeared in the door of the empty house. He had two collie dogs on leads in his hand.

Anna realized that this boy was the boy from the farm – the boy they had seen that morning with his sister playing on the rope. She had been right. Stephen had wanted to play with them but she had been right. She had known they were horrid.

Now she could see the girl, still in her jeans and boots, standing just behind her brother.

The boy seemed to be talking quietly to Stephen and the other boys. Anna couldn't hear what he was saying but it evidently calmed Stephen a little – perhaps he recognized the voice – for he stopped struggling and let the boys lead him blindfolded into the house.

Anna waited until they were out of sight, then she got up again, crossed the lane and walked quietly up the drive. A nettle brushed against her bare leg and she automatically looked for a dock leaf to soothe the stringing, but she could not see one.

She decided to go round behind the empty house and to see if she could look in the windows at the back. Fortunately there was a path. The bricks it had been made from were almost obscured by the grass that had sprung up between them, but at least there were no nettles or brambles and she got round unscathed.

The glass of the window was very dirty but Anna found she could see into the room if she pressed her face very close. She tangled with a spider's web and put her hand up to brush it away. Then she froze, fearful that the slight movement might have attracted attention to the face at the window. But the children inside the cottage were much too interested in their prisoner to be aware of anything going on outside.

The whole ground floor of the cottage seemed to be one big room, with a huge stone fireplace at one end. Anna could see Stephen, still blindfolded, standing with his back to the fireplace. From the way he was standing, Anna thought he looked as if he were saying to himself: 'All right. Do what you like. I'm not scared.'

The two boys who had sprung out at him stood one on either side, as if they would grab him if he made any attempt to escape. Each one held by its leash one of the dogs.

At the other end of the room some empty tea chests

had been piled on top of each other to form a rough platform and on top sat the boy from the farm. Below him, on another tea chest, sat his sister.

It was like a court scene. Anna had seen one on television. The boy from the farm seemed to have taken on the role of judge. Stephen was the prisoner in the dock. The other boys were the policemen. The girl was prosecuting. There was no defence.

As Anna watched, the girl took a bit of paper out of the pocket of her jeans and began to read:

'It is said that you on the 14th August did kidnap and wrongfully keep in your place of residence, *La Falaise*, Fleuron Bay, one kitten by the name of Gingerbread (Ginger for short) with intent to deprive his owners of him. Have you anything to say?'

'I don't know what on earth you mean,' Stephen said rather angrily, starting before the girl had quite finished. 'If the kitten's yours you could have had it any time you liked. We didn't kidnap him. He just liked us better than you and I'm not surprised.'

The boy in the judge's place said in a solemn voice: 'That will do. The judgment of the court is Guilty and the sentence is seven hours in prison with intent to deprive your parents of your presence as you deprived us of our kitten.'

'I wish you wouldn't use such long words,' Stephen said. 'You can't keep me in prison for seven hours. My parents would be terribly worried. It's not fair.'

'We were worried about the kitten,' the judge said. 'It seems fair to us. You had him longer than seven hours anyway.'

Anna thought they would shut Stephen up in the empty house, and that as soon as they'd gone she would be able to rescue him, but apparently the prison was somewhere else.

'We are not going to keep you here,' the judge said. 'Just in case, in spite of what we said about it being TOP SECRET, you told someone where you were going. You will come with us quietly. If you struggle it will be the worse for you. No one will interfere if they see us leading a blindfolded boy. They will think it is just a game.'

'And so it is a game,' Stephen said. 'You're just a lot of kids playing a game. But it's not a very good game because you don't keep to the rules. In a real trial the prisoner has someone speaking for him. You were all against me. And if you'd got any proper evidence you'd have known your kitten just took a fancy to us. I never kidnapped anyone in my life.'

'I'm sure you'll be more careful in future,' the judge said coldly. 'All right, chaps. Take him away.'

One of the 'policemen' opened the door with the hand that was not holding the dog, then they both walked out of the room with Stephen between them.

Anna, still looking through the window, knew that she had to follow them, to find out where they were taking Stephen. But she couldn't until the judge and his sister had left the cottage. She couldn't risk being taken prisoner as well, and she thought that they wouldn't hesitate to take her if they found her. Wasn't she as guilty as Stephen? More so really. At least Stephen had put the kitten up on the wall and had tried to encourage him to go home. But the message had been for Stephen. It had said at the top 'To the boy with the fair hair'. She wondered why.

The judge and his sister were still in the cottage. They had stacked the chests up against one wall so that the place no longer held its slight resemblance to a court room. Anna watched them through the window. She could see Stephen's black pullover lying on the floor by the fireplace. It looked a bit like a lean black cat curled up in front of the fire, but the grate was cold and the pullover was lifeless. She thought of that other cat, the ginger kitten, and how much trouble he had innocently caused them. Or had he? The judge and his sister certainly seemed to care about him, but had the trial really been as straightforward as it seemed? Hadn't it been a put-up job? Wasn't the kitten just an excuse for them to get hold of Stephen?

The boy and girl were talking quietly now down the far end of the room, and Anna couldn't hear what they were saying. At last they left the cottage and Anna could hear them running down the drive.

She took only a minute to dart into the cottage and rescue Stephen's pullover before following them, but when she came to the entrance of the drive there was no sign of them. She hesitated. Should she go right or left? There was no way of knowing. They had disappeared as surely as if she had imagined the whole thing.

Anna felt tears leap to her eyes. What was she to do? She could ask someone: 'Have you seen two boys with dogs and another one blindfolded between them?' 'Have you seen the boy and girl from the farm next to *La Falaise*?' She didn't know what it was called. Certainly these were questions she could ask. But there was no one to ask. And she couldn't just abandon Stephen, going home and saying casually 'Stephen will be out until ten o'clock tonight.' Seven hours was a terrible long time to be shut up by yourself with nothing to read and nothing to eat. It was unthinkable not to try to rescue him.

Then suddenly there swam into her mind for no apparent reason the map she had seen on the wall of Christopher Fisher's study, the map she had copied for the treasure hunt, and she realized, as she had not before, that one of the crosses on it had marked the empty cottage. It seemed possible, just possible, that one of the other crosses marked the prison Stephen had been taken to. At least it was worth trying and she could think of nothing else to do.

Anna had left her purse, with her own copy of the map in it, in her bedroom, not thinking she would be needing any money, or indeed the map. She didn't want to go into the house but she thought it would be easy enough to squeeze past the far side of the shed and go down to Christopher Fisher's study. On the original map she could check just exactly where the other two crosses were and then go and see if Stephen were imprisoned at either of them.

There seemed to be no one around. Perhaps her parents and Jenny were in the house. More likely they'd gone down to the beach again. Anna pushed open the door of the study, remembering she had forgotten to lock it the day before.

She pulled the chair over to the wall and stood on it so she could examine Christopher Fisher's map carefully. Yes, there they were – the three red crosses – and one certainly marked the empty house. She could see the turning by the mill, the mill itself marked with a circle. The other cross that was near *La Falaise* and seemed more likely to be the prison, was down another turning off the road to St Helier and nearer to the sea. It was the second turning on the left after the lane to the empty cottage.

Looking at the map, it seemed to her more and more likely that the second cross marked the prison. It would explain the extraordinary disappearance of the judge and his sister, for it was probable from the map that they could have got from the one cross to the other without going along roads. There was likely to be a gate into a field just farther up the lane from the cottage.

Anna was thinking these things and staring at the

map on the wall when she realized there was another piece of paper underneath it. The two pieces of typing paper had been pinned to the cork wall together and it was not surprising that she hadn't noticed them both the first time. Anna didn't hesitate. It seemed a very long time since her mother had told her not to touch anything (had it really been only yesterday?). And with Stephen in prison, such everyday instructions seemed hardly to apply.

Anna pulled out the drawing pins carefully and read the words on the piece of paper underneath:

'Convenient places for the disposal of bodies.
1 Empty cottage in Mill Lane.
2 Abandoned air-raid shelter on road to Bonjour Bay.
3 Cave to west of Fleuron Bay.'

Anna had read automatically to the bottom of the page. Now she read that first line again: 'Convenient places for the disposal of bodies.'

Her first feeling was one of disappointment. So the crosses had nothing to do with the Treasure at all.

Her second feeling was one of alarm. No wonder Mr Fisher had covered the second page with the map.

With her heart thumping, she thought of Stephen. No one was going to dispose of *his* body if she had anything to do with it. With the map in her hand, she rushed out of the study and yelled, 'Is anyone around?'

65

FIVE

A test passed

Even through the red scarf which served as a blindfold, Stephen could, of course, tell when they came out into the sunlight from the interior of the cottage. The dogs seemed to be straining at their leashes and pulling Stephen's escorts along, but it was difficult for him to walk quickly when he could not see and he stumbled several times on the rough drive before he felt the firmer surface of the lane beneath his sandals. They turned left away from the mill and the road to *La Falaise*, and only a minute later one of the boys let go the arm he was holding and Stephen could hear him opening a gate.

With only the one restraining hand on his arm, Stephen thought for a moment of pulling off his blindfold with his free hand and trying to escape. But he had not seen his guards and sensed that one of them, anyway, was both heavier and stronger than he was. Moreover, he was curious about where they were taking him and just what they meant to do with him. If he had to spend seven hours locked up in solitary confinement it would be rather unpleasant certainly.

He knew quite a number of poems by heart – they had rather an old-fashioned English master at school who believed in what he called 'stocking the imagination's larder with the fruit of the poets'. He also knew a lot of hymns – he was in the choir at church – and he could sing most of the tunes from *The Yellow Submarine* and the *Sound of Music*, two films he had seen recently. They would keep him occupied for quite a while and then he imagined, if the floor wasn't too hard, he might possibly sleep.

In any case, when it got to supper time and he still hadn't turned up, Anna would be bound to tell them about the note and his father would start looking for him. He had deliberately left his pullover on the floor of the cottage so that they would know he had been there. If only he had a reel of cotton to unwind like Theseus, wasn't it, in the Labyrinth; but even if he had had one, what could he have done blindfolded and guarded? The most he could do was to tread as firmly as possible on the field path, still a little yielding from the heavy rain of the morning before. He hoped his footmarks would show but his sandals were light and he doubted it.

What a lot of fuss these children were making about one small ginger kitten. Surely they must have realized that there had been no kidnapping, that the animal had come in of its own free will and stayed because it liked it, and had nothing better to do with its time. Heavens, he had even put it up on the wall to encourage it to go home, and they hadn't bribed it to stay with a saucer of milk, thanks to his mother.

No, the more he thought about it as he tramped as heavily as he could along the field path between his guards, trying to keep up with the eager dogs who were racing ahead as if they were hounds on the scent of a fox, the more he thought about it the more he considered it was a trumped-up charge, a cover for something else, a mere excuse to get him into their power. But why? What did they want from him?

One of his guards spoke for the first time since they had left the empty cottage. 'We're coming out on the road now. Just do as we say and you'll be all right. You have to get through a fence here.'

'Oh, can't I take off this wretched scarf,' Stephen said. 'I didn't blindfold your cat.'

'It's Denis's cat, not ours,' the boy said, pronouncing the name Denny, not rhyming it with tennis. 'We can't take your blindfold off. Orders is orders. Now get through here.' The two boys pushed Stephen between the wires they were holding apart, but it's difficult to judge anything when you can't see and Stephen managed to catch the back of his neck on the barbed wire. He wanted instinctively to put his hand up to it but his arms were pinned to his side again. It didn't hurt much but he could feel the warm blood trickling down his neck and cooling as it ran down inside his shirt.

They walked along the road in silence. Only one

car passed and it appeared to find nothing odd in the sight of the three boys and the two dogs, for after hooting at them to get into the side it continued its way without pausing.

'I could have shouted out,' Stephen thought, as the sound of the car died away in the distance. But he hadn't wanted to. This was something he had to handle by himself. He really began to hope that Anna would not show the note to their parents, that there would not be a search party.

'Down here,' said the same guard who had spoken before. 'It's not far now.'

'What is *it*?' Stephen asked, conversationally.

'The prison, of course,' the boy said.

As before when he had come out into the light, so now as he went into the darkness, Stephen could see it blindfolded. But this seemed real darkness, not dimness. There was a strange musty, airless smell and he could feel earth beneath his sandals. What sort of place had they found for him?

'Sit down,' said the boy who did all the talking. 'Here.' He helped Stephen to find a wooden box.

'What happens now?' Stephen asked.

A voice came out of the darkness – Denis's voice. He and his sister, unencumbered by a blindfolded prisoner, must have got to the prison more quickly; they must have overtaken them silently on the way. It was quite possible of course, but it had the effect Denis had wanted.

Stephen was startled and impressed.

Denis said: 'You have come to your destination. We shall now leave you in solitary confinement for the prescribed sentence of seven hours. At the end of that time you will hear an alarm bell ring and you will find the doors are open and you can walk out. Before that time there is no point in trying to escape. No one can escape from this prison. Au revoir.'

They had gone. Stephen could no longer hear the dogs' panting breaths. It was quiet but *had* they all gone? Somehow Stephen did not feel alone. Of course, there was a clock ticking – the alarm clock which would tell him when seven hours had passed.

He tore off his blindfold but could see nothing. The place he was in – whatever it was – was in complete darkness. The only things he could see were the faint luminous numbers on the face of the clock. It was ten past three.

He shivered, from cold not fear, and wished he had not left his pullover in the empty cottage. It was very cold in this place, so cold that surely he must be under the earth. That would account for the smell, too. He stood up and felt the boundaries of his prison with his hands. It seemed to be a curved structure of corrugated iron with doors at both ends and no windows at all. Supposing he suffocated, that would teach them to get up to such idiotic tricks. Manslaughter, he supposed, would be the charge brought against them.

But Denis seemed far too competent a person to

make such an elementary mistake. There must be a ventilator somewhere. Stephen ran his hands right along the top of his prison. It was not very high and it was easy enough for him to reach. He felt a slight irregularity in the ribcage and saw far above him, as if he were looking up a long pipe, some tiny chinks of blue sky. He breathed deeply and immediately felt much better.

So it was just a question of enduring the seven hours. His feet knocked against the wooden box and he sat down again. What was he going to do with all this time? Exploring the limits of his space and looking for the ventilator had, he discovered, looking at the luminous dial of the clock, taken only five minutes. It seemed the longest five minutes he could ever remember. And it was just twelve minutes since he'd taken off the blindfold. Six hours and forty-eight minutes to go. How was he to keep sane?

'Is there anyone around?' Anna called again in panic, running across the garden.

A window upstairs opened wider and her father put his head out. 'What on earth's the matter, Anna? Can't I have forty winks without . . .'

'Oh, do come quickly, Pa, please. It's urgent. Honestly it is.'

Luke Simpson took one look at Anna's white face and said, 'All right. Hang on. I'll be down in two minutes.'

He pulled his trousers on, shoved his feet into his shoes and ran down the stairs. Anna was sitting on the kitchen doorstep with her head in her hands. Her father got a glass and filled it at the tap.

'Here, drink this and then tell me what it's all about.'

Anna drank. While she drank, her father talked normally. 'Jenny and your mother have gone down to the beach again. I thought I'd put my feet up. We wondered where you and Stephen had got to. Where is he?'

'That's just the point. I don't know what's happened to him but I think I know where he is. Oh, do come with me. I've got a map. I'm sure he's in danger.'

Her father let her take his hand and lead him away from the house. He tried to get more sense out of her, but by this time the words TOP SECRET had swum into Anna's mind again and she seemed terrified to say any more.

As they walked along the road, Anna clung to her father's hand and said nothing. Luke Simpson stopped asking questions. So they walked, quickly and in silence, past the farm and the shop and the turning to the empty cottage until they came to the junction where one road curved down towards Fleuron Bay and the other to St Helier. 'Down here,' Anna said, and they took the St Helier road, turning off it a few minutes later when the signpost pointed to Bonjour Bay.

'I think that's the place,' Anna said. The road at this point had been cut out of the hillside and the fields on the left hand side were seven or eight feet above the road. Into this bank there was a square cut doorway edged with cement, just high enough for a man to enter stooping a little. A boy would not need to stoop at all.

'What's going on?' her father asked, puzzled. 'That's an old air-raid shelter, Anna, left over from the war.' As they came nearer the entrance to the shelter, they could hear voices.

'Is Stephen there?'

'Yes, I'm sure he is,' Anna said. 'Oh, see if he's all right.'

'He sounds all right to me,' her father said. 'Do you think we should interrupt?'

'Oh yes, oh yes,' Anna said. She had become so accustomed in the last half hour to the idea that Stephen was in deadly danger that her ears were unable to convince her that the noise she heard was a happy noise.

Alone in the pitch dark of the old air-raid shelter, Stephen had wondered how he could possibly keep sane for six hours and forty-eight minutes. Singing, of course, as he'd thought on the way, would help a good deal. He had started off with his favourite hymn, his voice sounding rather good, he thought, as it reverberated in the confined space.

'Let all the world in every corner sing,
My God and King!
The heavens are not too high,
His praise may thither fly:
The earth is not too low,
His praises there may grow . . .'

Stephen broke off. Surely that was a sound he'd heard. Yes, there was a long streak of light down the edge of the door, and then more light, and silhouetted against it, the figure of a boy with the bright eye of a torch in his hand.

'All right, it's all over,' Denis said. 'You've passed.'

'I'm Yvonne,' the girl said, following her brother into the underground shelter. 'We've taken the dogs back to the farm. There's not enough room for them really.'

The other two boys came in. 'I'm Gerard,' the bigger one said.

Stephen recognized his voice.

'I'm Marc,' the smaller one said. Stephen had not heard him talk before.

'What is all this about?' Stephen asked. 'What do you mean, it's all over? What have I passed?'

'We're sorry it had to be like this,' Denis said. He really sounded sorry. His voice and manner had completely changed. 'But we had to find out what you were like, you see. We *thought* you looked our sort but we couldn't be sure. You can never really tell by

74

appearances. So we put you through a sort of Test, to see how you'd stand up to it.'

'We had Tests, too, before we were allowed to join,' Gerard said.

'Join what?' Stephen asked dully. 'Why should I want to join you when you've treated me like this?'

They were standing around uncomfortably. Now Yvonne knelt down on the floor and spread out a rug. Stephen noticed that the boys were all carrying things, too. By the light of the torch they began to unpack. They took out jam-jars and set up in them fat white candles, digging the jars into the earth floor so that they wouldn't be knocked over.

Stephen saw that they had brought a feast with them – bread and raspberry jam and chocolate biscuits and apples and milk.

Stephen repeated himself but in a friendlier way. The food looked very good and the room, which had irked him before with its small darkness, now seemed in the candlelight, exciting and mysterious. 'Why do you think I want to join your club or whatever it is?'

'Because you'll have a better holiday if you do,' Denis said simply. 'It was obvious to us that you didn't want to spend the whole time in Jersey with no one to do things with but your sisters – one a stuck-up prig and the other a baby.'

'Oh, they're all right really,' Stephen said loyally. 'Anna's all right. She just doesn't like things that get you dirty. She loves everything to be pretty and clean and easy. . . . It does get a bit boring.' He didn't know about the treasure hunt.

'Have some bread and jam,' Yvonne said, with her mouth full.

'What do I have to do now?' Stephen asked, taking a piece.

'Oh, nothing,' Denis said. 'You just do the things we do – we don't have rules or any of that nonsense. Except not to give away the secret of the Test.'

'Okay,' Stephen said. They all shook hands and started to talk at once.

Stephen was asking where they were, what this place was that they were in. Marc and Gerard were trying to explain together about it being an air-raid shelter built under a field in the Second World War before Jersey was occupied by the Germans. Yvonne was asking Stephen if he wanted some milk. Denis was saying they'd have to be getting along soon because he had to help with the milking.

The noise was tremendous when the door suddenly burst open and there was, for a moment, complete silence.

When Anna saw Stephen with a piece of bread and jam in his hand in the flickering candlelight she felt not relief but betrayal.

'Are you all right, son?' Luke Simpson spoke first. 'We were wondering where you'd got to.'

'Of course I'm all right, Pa,' Stephen said. 'These

are my friends. How did you find me?' He looked genuinely astonished and Anna realized that of course he didn't know she had watched the trial scene in the cottage, that she had guessed he might have been taken to the air-raid shelter and that she had feared from the note on Christopher Fisher's wall that Stephen had somehow got mixed up in something really sinister.

Stephen did not know she knew anything of what he had been through. However much he might make light of it now, Anna knew it had been an ordeal for him. If he wanted their father to know nothing about it, all right, she could act too.

'We just happened to be walking down the lane. We were going to Bonjour Bay,' she added, to make it sound convincing. 'And we heard the noise you were making and recognized Stephen's voice.'

Their father seemed prepared to let this story stand. He knew Anna was embarrassed at having been so needlessly upset. 'We'd been wondering where you were,' he said. 'So naturally we came in. But we'll be getting along now we know you're with friends.'

'I'll be home for supper,' Stephen said, thinking to himself how he'd imagined he might not be.

Anna couldn't talk on the way back to *La Falaise*. She was very near to tears. Still clutching the map in one hand, she held her father's hand with the other. How could Stephen be such a turncoat? She had heard the words in a history lesson at school and it fitted exactly. He had gone over to the enemy. But why? What extraordinary thing had happened in that short half hour which had passed from the time she had seen him marched blindfolded out of the empty cottage, guarded by boys and dogs, to the moment when they had opened the door of the air-raid shelter? Anna could not imagine, and she had an awful feeling Stephen would never tell her. Only boys could behave like that. That girl was as bad as a boy in her dirty jeans and boots. Anna shuddered.

'Is there anything you want to tell me?' her father asked gently.

'No,' Anna said. She would not tell Stephen's secret. But there was one thing, wasn't there, the worst thing of all, that now, it seemed, had nothing to do with either the treasure or Stephen. She could tell her father about the map and the hidden notes.

'There is one thing,' Anna said. 'This map which led us to the shelter. . . .'

'Yes, I wondered about that,' Luke Simpson said. 'Where did you get it from?'

'I got it from Christopher Fisher's study,' Anna admitted. 'And there's a note on the wall – it was hidden under the map but I took it off and discovered it.' She swallowed. Her mouth felt dry. 'It was about the best places for disposing of bodies.'

It was then that her father began to laugh. Although he knew what Anna had been feeling, he couldn't stop himself, and the lane echoed with his laughing. Some people passing in a car looked curiously at him.

When he had calmed down a bit, Anna said rather coldly, 'What was all that about? What's so funny about that?'

'Oh darling, I am sorry. I shouldn't have laughed. I know you've had a fright. But it's all right. It's all right. There's nothing to worry about. No real bodies are going to be disposed of. Christopher Fisher's a thriller writer, you know. You'd forgotten that, had you? He writes stories about murders. He was obviously making some notes and plans for his next book.'

Anna smiled weakly. 'I'll put the map back on his wall,' he said. 'It's still quite clean.'

SIX

Finding Felicity

Waking up next morning, it took Anna a moment to realize why she felt so miserable. Instead of reaching for her book, she tried to burrow more deeply under her bedclothes and go to sleep again. But it was no good. All the things that had happened yesterday afternoon crowded into her mind.

Jenny started singing, and Anna said, 'Oh, be quiet, Jenny,' crossly, and then felt even more miserable because she knew it wasn't Jenny she was angry with. It was herself, for being so stupid about Christopher Fisher's map, and it was Stephen for making friends with the farm children, and it was the farm children themselves for being tough and rough, and for taking Stephen away from her.

Then she felt a bit better as she remembered Felicity, and the fact that it was this morning they were to go treasure hunting together. Of course, without the map it would be a needle in a haystack business. But at least there *was* still a treasure to be looked for. Nothing could take away those words, that message, that Victoria Fisher had left for her. 'WATCH OUT FOR THE

ONLY TREASURE.' It would still be worth exploring the caves to the west of the bay.

Felicity had told Anna to be at the hotel about ten. Looking at her watch, Anna suddenly remembered today was her parents' wedding anniversary. She jumped out of bed. Jenny was standing up in the cot looking interested. So Anna gave her a pile of books and told her not to disturb their mother and father.

'For once,' Anna said. Jenny was inclined to wake her parents up in the morning by bouncing on their bed or shouting in their ears some vital piece of news.

Anna went downstairs to make a cup of tea as a sort of wedding anniversary present. Before leaving England she had bought a beautiful card with flowers and lace and things on it, and she'd got Stephen to sign it and Jenny to do a rather wobbly 'J'.

She was in a hurry, fearing that if she didn't get the tea upstairs soon, her parents would be out of bed and the whole point lost. She poured herself a cup first to test it and it was just as well she did. She hadn't let the kettle boil properly and the tea was hardly tea at all, more a nasty brand of hot water and milk. She poured the whole lot down the sink and started again.

She put four biscuits on the tray. Stephen could come down and get his own if he wanted one. Last night, when he came in just before supper, Anna had been about to tell him she had watched his trial but it was obvious that he didn't want to talk to her. Well, if he wanted to spend all his time with those beastly children, he could. At least she had Felicity.

Anna propped the card up against the teapot. Upstairs, she knocked quietly against the door with the front of the tray and walked into her parents' bedroom.

'Many happy returns of your wedding day. Is that what you say?'

'Oh thank you, thank you. Tea – how lovely.' Her mother sat up and stretched herself. Her father just pulled the blanket over his head.

'I wish I could get married,' Anna said. 'I wish I could miss out all that school and having jobs and things. I can't think there'd ever be anyone I'd want to marry but I'd love to have a little house of my own and a ginger kitten and twins aged one called Charlotte and Jonathan. They'd look awfully sweet learning to walk.'

Her mother laughed. 'They wouldn't be one all the time, you know. They'd get to be as big as Stephen in no time at all. Tea, Luke.' She had poured out his cup and gave it to Anna to put on his side of the bed.

He surfaced and shook himself, like a dog coming out of a pond. 'Mm. That's nice,' he said appreciatively. 'A Red Letter Day with early morning tea by Miss Anna Simpson.'

'Well, it's white not red,' Anna said, giving him the envelope.

'Good heavens, what's this? Is it really our wedding anniversary? I'd forgotten all about it. Fourteen years. Good heavens!'

'It's nice to have someone who remembers,' his wife said.

'I put it in my birthday book,' Anna explained, between mouthfuls of biscuit. 'And I've got a better present for you than the card or tea.' It had come to her as they were talking. 'You can have a free day. You can go somewhere in the car by yourselves. I'll look after Jenny and give her lunch. And Stephen – well, he's going off with those horrible new friends of his.'

'Are you sure you can manage? It's a lovely idea. We could go to that seafood place at Rozel and have lobsters. It'd be far too expensive for all of us but . . .'

Anna left them happily discussing their plans for the day and realized, as she took Jenny's biscuit into her, that her unselfish impulse had rather ruined her own plans. She would have to take Jenny with her to meet Felicity and to go treasure hunting.

Anna smiled at Fred as she walked up the hotel steps with Jenny. He'd just finished serving someone and came over to them.

'Orange juice for two, is it, today?' he asked.

'No, not today, thank you. Have you seen Felicity? I'm meeting her at ten.'

'Well, ten it is, miss,' Fred said, looking at his watch. 'I should ask at the desk, if I was you. I've not set eyes on Miss Felicity this morning myself. She hasn't favoured me with her presence, that I can say.'

''Ave some orange juice,' Jenny said.

'No, we're going inside.'

The woman at the desk said she didn't know where Miss Felicity was either. She admired her own painted finger nails and went on reading the paper.

Anna and Jenny just stood there, not knowing what to do.

''Ave some orange juice,' Jenny said again.

'Drinks outside on the terrace,' the woman said in a very superior voice, hardly looking up from her paper.

'Could I, do you think it would be possible, could I speak to Mrs Le Brun?' Anna asked hesitantly.

'She's very busy in the office this time of the morning,' the woman said.

Anna decided to go and see if Felicity was in her room. It seemed the most likely place for her to be. She went upstairs holding Jenny's hand and came to the door marked PRIVATE. She knocked and when there was no reply she pushed and went in, just in case Felicity had left a note for her.

The room was empty except for the poodles. Jenny wanted to stay and play with them but Anna felt guilty, sure that someone would come along any moment and accuse her of being on private property. She took a last look round the room. It was very tidy with everything in its place and no sign of a note anywhere.

'Come on,' she said to Jenny. She had noticed the door marked OFFICE at the other end of the hall from the reception room. She put her fingers to her lips. Jenny asked 'Why?' loudly, but the woman at the desk didn't look up. Anna knocked at the office door. After all, Felicity had told her to meet her at ten. What could have happened to her? Could she have had an accident in the surf at St Ouen's yesterday afternoon?

'Come in,' a voice said, rather impatiently, as if it would have liked to add 'if you must'.

'I'm very sorry to interrupt you,' Anna began, putting her head round the door.

'Oh, come in,' Mrs Le Brun said. 'It's no good being half in and half out. Oh, there are two of you, are there? What's it all about? Wait a minute, I've seen you before somewhere, haven't I?'

'Yes, you saw me with Felicity yesterday. And she told me to meet her here at ten today, and I can't find her anywhere.'

'Oh, I am sorry. How tiresome for you. But that is just a wee bit like our darling Felicity, I'm afraid. I wonder where she is?'

'I thought something awful might have happened to her. She told me she was going surfing at St Ouen's yesterday.'

'Yes, of course, with Suzanne Renouf. She got back all right at about eight. Let me see.' Mrs Le Brun went over to a huge calendar hanging on the wall. 'Here we are. It's Saturday the 17th today – oh yes, of course, it's the Fleuron Manor Horse Show. She'll be up at the Manor.'

'But she told me to meet her here,' Anna said. She couldn't believe it. 'She told me to come about ten.'

'Want to go home,' Jenny said.

'Well, I'm awfully sorry, my pets. It really is too bad of Felicity and I shall tell her so when I see her, the darling. In the meantime, I'm afraid I'll have to say goodbye. I've got a wee pile of work waiting for me.'

'Yes, of course,' Anna said, politely. 'Come on, Jenny.' She closed the door softly behind them.

'Well, that's that,' she said gloomily.

They were going down the steps when Fred called from the terrace. 'Find her, did you?'

'No, she's gone to the Horse Show, her mother said.'

'Oh yes, of course. Might have told you that myself if I'd of thought.'

'Have thought,' Anna said automatically. It was what her father said when she made the same mistake. 'Oh, I'm sorry. Go on.'

Fred looked a bit put out but he went on, 'Not a bad place to go to on a nice sunny morning. Do you fancy it yourself then?'

'Well . . . oh yes. I hadn't thought.' Jenny might like horses. It was a good idea. And she could find Felicity and perhaps they could go treasure hunting after all. 'Where is it?'

Fred told them how to find Fleuron Manor. 'You can take a short cut across the beach. You can see the bottom of the road over there.'

'Want some orange juice,' Jenny said as they left the hotel.

There was a kiosk selling things at the edge of the

beach. 'All right, you can have something nice to cheer you up,' Anna said. 'What do you want?'

'A bird's nest with a bird in it,' Jenny said. She seemed to have forgotten about the orange juice.

'No, I mean something we can buy,' Anna said.

'A balloon,' said Jenny, pointing to an inflatable swimming ring.

'That's not a balloon,' Anna said.

'I call it a balloon because you blow it up,' Jenny said.

'It's too expensive anyway. How about an ice lolly? Not the dripping kind, though. I don't want you looking a mess when we see Felicity.'

They crossed the beach, both sucking their ice lollies.

'Help!' shrieked Jenny. A dog was jumping up at her.

'Oh, it's all right,' Anna said, shooing the dog away. 'He just wanted your ice lolly. He was probably hot. Nobody buys him ice lollies, you see.'

'Oh no, of course not,' Jenny said, cheering up. 'Cos he hasn't got hands to hold one, has he?' She licked her lolly with renewed pleasure.

It was quite a long walk up to Fleuron Manor. They stopped to rest at a gate into a field. There were quiet cows munching the grass.

'I like cows better than dogs. And tortoises,' Jenny said. The cows looked at them with mild brown eyes and then went on munching.

Half way up the hill Jenny said, 'Want Mummy.'
Anna had to carry her on her back for the rest of the
way. She was quite heavy for the steep slope and her
arms felt tight round Anna's neck. Anna was glad
when they came to the yellow AA sign FLEURON
MANOR and the one beside it saying HORSE LINES, with
an arrow.

There was a man at the gates in a sort of sentry box.
'One and six for kids,' he said, then seeing the look on
Anna's face, he added, 'We'll say we haven't seen the
little one.'

'Oh, thank you,' Anna said, putting down one and
six. 'Has it started yet?'

'Oh dear me, yes. They've been carrying on in the rings since 9 o'clock. There's a lot to get through,' he said. 'And it's likely to rain.'

Anna looked up and noticed for the first time that there were indeed dark clouds piling up on one side of the sky, though the grounds of the Manor were still in sunshine.

'I wonder where Felicity is,' Anna said to Jenny. There was a fun fair to the left of the drive with a band playing loud pop music. 'I shouldn't think she'd be there.'

'I want a go on the aboutaround,' Jenny said.

'No, you can't go on the roundabout,' Anna said. 'We want to find Felicity. We want to look for the Treasure, don't we?'

'What's treasure?' Jenny asked, looking over her shoulder and watching the roundabout twirling, laden with small girls and boys.

'It's something worth a lot. Something you value a lot,' Anna said. Jenny looked blank. She wasn't really listening.

There was suddenly a burst of clapping from the direction of the show ring.

'Come on, Jenny, let's see the horses.'

'I like cows better than horses,' Jenny said. 'And tortoises.'

'No, horses are nice,' Anna said patiently.

'Eat my tummy,' Jenny said, looking back at the roundabout.

'The horses won't eat your tummy. I won't let them.'
They came up to the ring and found a spare seat at the
end of a bench. Anna sat down and pulled Jenny on to
her knee. Galloping music came out of a loudspeaker
just above their heads.

In the ring a lot of children on horseback were
galloping round a number of poles that had been stuck
into the ground. When the music stopped they each
had to try to steer their horses to an empty pole and
put their riding hats on top. One boy rashly threw his
at a pole and when it missed a girl rode up calmly and
put hers on instead. The boy jumped down to retrieve
his hat but he was too late. All the poles were taken and
he had to leave the ring.

A man with a straw hat on and a large rosette in his
buttonhole came up and removed a pole. Then the
music started again and the whole thing was repeated.
Anna clapped loudly when at last the winner was clear
– a rather thin girl with fair plaits and a jacket that was
a bit small for her.

'She was very good, wasn't she?' Anna said. She
had been so interested in watching Musical Hats that
she had forgotten to look for Felicity. Now she stood
up and looked all long the benches that lined the ring.
There was no sign of her.

Now another event was starting. A voice boomed
over the loudspeaker: 'CLASS 12. 12.2 hands OPEN
JUMPING. Registered ponies ridden by registered members born in or after 1955.' Then the voice read out a

long list of horses and riders with their numbers. What odd names some of the horses had: Ginger Snap of Nashead: Briarwood Pop-A-Long: Sherberton Maypole. Imagine calling out names like those! Probably they used shortened versions: Ginger and Briar and Sherbie. But what about 'Benjamin Bunny'? Fancy calling a horse after a rabbit. It didn't seem possible. As each horse was named he trotted into the ring.

Anna was thinking idly like this when the loud-speaker voice said clearly 'No. 74. Dunbarton Star, ridden by Miss Felicity Le Brun.' Anna couldn't believe her ears. So that's what Mrs Le Brun had meant when she said Felicity would be 'up at the Manor'. And here Felicity was – perfectly turned-out as usual and on a perfectly turned-out horse. Some of the other children wore corduroy trousers or even denim jeans with light pullovers, but Felicity, of course, had beautifully-cut jodhpurs, a black jacket and black velvet hat with her fair hair swinging smoothly below it.

Anna sighed. Felicity looked so beautiful and remote. How could Anna hope to interest this girl, who took part in pageants, water-skied, and rode horseback, in probing around in some caves for a treasure which might not even exist?

'WATCH OUT FOR THE ONLY TREASURE.' That word 'only' was odd. What had Victoria Fisher meant by it? Naturally there would be only one. No one would expect to find two.

All the horses had trotted round the ring once while the names were being read out. Now they were waiting patiently at the far end of the ring, swishing the flies away with their tails.

The jumping began. Some of the horses made it look very easy – sailing over the jumps as if they had wings. Others didn't like it at all and refused to have anything to do with it – coming to a full stop each time a few feet away from the jump and tossing their heads. At the

third refusal they had to leave the ring with their young owners blushing and confused.

At last it was time for Dunbarton Star and Felicity. They cleared the first two jumps with ease but at the third one the top bar trembled and fell to the ground. At the fifth the horse refused the first time and only just cleared it the second. At the sixth, the one that looked like a wall, Dunbarton Star's hind legs dislodged one of the bricks. 'Eleven faults,' the loudspeaker boomed as Felicity rode out of the ring. She looked extremely cross and gave her horse what might have been a pat but looked more like a smack.

Anna was sad for her. It was a pity she couldn't perform as beautifully as she looked.

'Let's go and see Felicity,' Anna said, getting up and putting Jenny on her feet.

They found her bending over and giving her shoes a polish. Dunbarton Star cropped apologetically at the long grass growing beneath the trees at the end of the field.

'Hullo, Felicity,' Anna said.

'Oh, hullo,' Felicity said, rather unenthusiastically, straightening up after a last rub at her shoes.

'Eat my tummy,' Jenny said, eyeing Dunbarton Star suspiciously.

'He prefers grass,' Anna said. 'He's a lovely horse, Felicity.'

'Yes, but we had a rotten round. Did you see it?'

Anna nodded, though she realized Felicity wished

she hadn't. Then she said: 'You said we could go to the caves today.'

Felicity shrugged her shoulders. 'Did I? I must have forgotten about the Show. How silly of me.'

'Could you come later on?' Anna asked.

'No, not today,' Felicity said. 'I've got five more events.'

Anna swallowed. Felicity hadn't even said sorry. Well, she and Jenny would go by themselves. If Felicity would tell them the way.

'Go aboutaround,' Jenny said hopefully, but no one took any notice.

'How do we get to the caves?' Anna asked.

Felicity took a notebook and pencil out of the pocket of her jacket and drew a map.

'The most difficult part is the beginning. You have to get round a point just beyond the bay where it doesn't look as if it could possibly lead anywhere. Once you're round that it's not too bad. You just have to keep going until you find them. There are only two. Most people don't go any farther than the first. The rocks are very slippery with seaweed. If there's anything there it's likely to be in the farthest one. I must say I'd think it was some silly game of those Fisher kids if it wasn't for the map you said their father had made.'

Anna didn't tell her that that map had turned out to refer to other things. She just said, 'I like caves anyhow.'

The voice was booming out of the loudspeaker again: 'CLASS 14. JUNIOR TROTTING RACE. Ponies ridden by registered members born in or after 1957.'

'We've got to go,' Felicity said, giving Anna the bit of paper she'd drawn on. The voice began to read out the list of names: Elphicks Master William; Twylands Lonely Breeze; Mainoaks Sunflower; Brown Mouse.

How could you call a horse a mouse! What silly names! Anna thought. 'Come on, Jenny,' she said.

SEVEN

The caves

'Let's go home,' Jenny said, as they came out of the gates of Fleuron Manor.

Anna was really regretting her kind offer to her parents. Without Jenny she could have quickly run down the hill to the Bay again. With Jenny everything seemed impossible. But she had promised her parents she would look after Jenny and she had promised herself she would look for the treasure. She was determined to keep both promises.

They stood hesitating in the lane – to the right was the way down to the beach, to the left the gate into the tomato field and the short cut to *La Falaise*.

It was warm and still in the lane after the noise and movement of the Horse Show. They could still hear in the background the music from the fair and the heavy loudspeaker voice, but it only seemed to emphasize the quietness outside the grounds. A butterfly hovered over the scarlet pimpernels. The lane was edged with trees at this point, their trunks covered in ivy. Even the shadows seemed green.

Anna idly pulled off a piece of ivy and wound a tendril round her small finger like a ring. Jenny was jumping up and down impatiently.

'Want some orange juice,' Jenny said.

'All right,' Anna made up her mind. 'We'll go home now and you can have some orange juice and something to eat and a bit of a rest. Then we'll borrow Simon Fisher's pushchair and go down to the Bay again.'

They walked along the track between the tomato fields. It was still muddy after Thursday's rain.

'It's all buttery,' Jenny said, sliding on an oozing patch.

'Well, don't fall over,' Anna said, taking her hand.

When they got back to *La Falaise* they found a note from Stephen on the kitchen table.

HAVING LUNCH WITH FRIENDS.
SEE YOU LATER, ALLIGATOR.

Anna tore it up into little pieces and dropped it in the wastepaper basket. She poured Jenny a glass of orange juice and had one herself. Then she made some sandwiches for their lunch. Fortunately there was a sliced loaf. Anna wasn't very good at cutting bread. She gave Jenny a banana to keep her going and read her the whole of *Little Black Quasha* while she was sitting on her pot.

Then Anna decided it was time they went treasure-hunting. She packed the sandwiches, a bottle of orange juice, and a torch she'd found in the garage into a duffle bag and slung it over the back of Simon Fisher's pushchair. She noticed there was a grubby BEA label tied on it with the name Fisher written in ball pen. That must have been left there from the last time they went to England.

Jenny didn't want to go at first because she was sure they would meet a crocodile or a snake, like poor little Black Quasha. She said she liked cows better. And tortoises. Anna assured her they would be far more likely to meet cows than crocodiles. In fact, she said, there aren't any crocodiles in Jersey.

'How do you know?' Jenny asked. She still wouldn't get into the pushchair.

'Well, I haven't seen any,' Anna said.

'But you haven't been to the caves,' Jenny said. 'There might be crocodiles in the caves.'

'No, the books say there aren't any crocodiles in Jersey,' Anna said patiently.

Jenny was content with this. She believed in books. At last she agreed to climb into the pushchair.

Anna was pushing her out of the drive when she noticed that the black storm clouds were covering more of the sky.

'I'd better go back for our anoraks.'

At last they were moving along the lane. Jenny laughed and squealed as Anna pushed her rapidly over the rough surface. It had been a good idea to bring the pushchair even though it meant going the long way round by the road. Jenny's short legs would have enough to do when they got down to the shore.

Passing the farm, Anna had a glimpse of Stephen on the barn roof with some of his new friends. She waved but he didn't see her and she didn't call out.

They went quickly down the hill they had trudged up so slowly by the other road two hours earlier on the way to the Horse Show. They went down the village street. It was almost deserted. Perhaps everyone had gone to the Horse Show. Bunches of beach balls and sandshoes hung forlornly outside the shops. No one looked at the racks of postcards with photographs of Fleuron Bay from a dozen different angles.

When they came out on the front, Anna saw that the few people on the beach were packing up their things. A man in a yachting cap was folding up deckchairs and stacking them beneath the jetty. On the terrace of the Fleuron Bay Hotel the two women she had seen the morning before were putting away their knitting. In the doorway behind them she could see Fred hovering and looking up at the sky.

Anna stopped by a notice that said PARKING FOR FISHERMEN ONLY. There was another notice underneath it, but she didn't read it. She stood with her hand on the handle of the pushchair and looked out to sea. A seagull rode up and down on the prow of a small motor-boat. In another boat a fisherman was stowing his nets away. Then Jenny stood up in the pushchair and shrieked. Two frogmen were coming up out of the sea.

They looked like men from another world, laden with their bits and pieces like the White Knight in *Alice through the Looking Glass*. Their black rubber suits had yellow stripes down the arms and legs. There were weights round their waists and knives and oxygen cylinders on their backs. There were great waterproof watches on their wrists. Pipes from their cylinders ran into either side of their face masks. They looked very frightening.

Jenny was still crying. She seemed to think they were worse than crocodiles until Anna assured her they were only men specially dressed up for swimming underwater.

'They won't eat you, you can be sure of that,' she said. She pulled out of the pocket of her shorts the scrap of paper Felicity had drawn on.

'This is the way, Jenny.' The houses came to an end just past the harbour wall and the road ended there, too. But there was a track that ran along the coast and it was this that Felicity had told them they must follow for the caves. Anna found it easier to pull the push-chair rather than push it.

'You've got a pullchair now,' she said to Jenny, and Jenny was delighted with the new word and chanted if after her:

'Pull chair, Pull chair, Pull chair.'

At last the track got too rough even for pulling, but in any case Anna could see from Felicity's sketch map that they had reached the point where they would have to leave the track and drop down on to the rocks. If they followed the track they would end up on the top of the cliff, high above the sea and the caves.

Anna folded the pushchair and left it beside the track. There was nothing to hide it under and she hoped no one would come along and take it. Simon Fisher's name on the BEA label flapped in the slight wind coming from the sea.

Anna shivered a little. The wind was bringing the black clouds across the sky and the sun was almost obscured by them. They put their anoraks on and Anna slung the duffle bag over one shoulder.

'Come on,' she said to Jenny. She thought how silly it was to go treasure hunting with a three-year-old. She supposed she could have waited for tomorrow but why should she wait and wait just because Felicity was doing something else. Tomorrow she'd probably be going iceskating or flying or something, she thought resentfully, as she helped Jenny over the rocks.

At first she nearly turned back. She couldn't believe it was possible to get over one particularly large boulder without falling into the sea, but she remembered what Felicity had said about the first bit being the most difficult. And it was true. When at last she and Jenny and the bag were safely over the obstacle it was quite easy. The rocks were flat-topped and smooth, and it was simple to jump from one to another, stopping sometimes to look into rock pools and poke gently at the sea anemones.

They kept to the dry rocks covered in sea pinks above the high tide, as the wet rocks lower down were slippery with seaweed. But then they came to a place where there wasn't any dry rock. The cliff rose sheer above the wet rock.

'Careful here, Jenny,' Anna said. She was holding her sister's hand but even so the small girl skidded on the wet seaweed and fell, wedging herself awkwardly between one rock and the next. She began to cry. Her sobs got worse when she saw a slight trickle of blood down one leg where she had grazed it on a rough edge of the rock.

'It's all right, Jen,' Anna said, dabbing at the blood with a bit of Kleenex she had in her pocket. 'We're nearly there, honestly. Then we might find the treasure.' Suddenly it seemed very unlikely. 'Well, we'll have our sandwiches, anyway.'

There was a steep drop from the rock they were on down to a narrow gully of smooth, wet sand.

'I'll have to jump down first and then you can jump into my arms.' Jenny didn't object. She liked jumping. She often did it at home from the stairs.

When they were both down on the sand, Anna could see that there was a cave at the end of the gully, a dark mysterious hole under the cliff.

'It's the first cave,' she said. 'Come on, Jenny.'

It was a cave but it was a very shallow one and obviously one that had been frequently visited. People had carved their initials in the rock, and there was a

cigarette packet wedged under a stone. Anna, who had been wanting to feel as if she was treading where no foot had trod before, felt irritated.

'Let's go on,' she said to Jenny.

'Sandwiches,' Jenny said.

'Not in this cave,' Anna said. 'It's all wet anyway.' This was true. It was clear that the tide came right into the cave. Indeed, it was not very far away now. Anna climbed hurriedly up on to the rocks at the far side of the little inlet as a particularly big wave came rushing down towards the cave.

'I think the tide's coming in,' Anna said.

'Does the washing,' Jenny said.

'Oh, it's not that sort of Tide. It's just the sea. It comes up and down at different times. I think it's something to do with the moon,' Anna said vaguely.

They clambered over the next rocks. At this point there was a larger distance between the cliff face and the sea so they were able to keep to the dry rocks. Anna noticed how many different kinds of lichen there were, so that no two rocks looked the same colour. But they all looked dull, for the sun had gone in and the whole sky was dark.

'Sandwiches,' Jenny said again.

At that moment it began it rain – slow, large spots of it that splashed down on the dry rocks in wet circles until rapidly the whole surface was wet.

'We'd better go back,' Anna said. They pulled up their anorak hoods and turned round. Jenny started to cry a little, very quietly.

When they came to the narrow inlet with the cave at the end they found their way was blocked. The sand they had walked over such a short time before was full of rushing water. Anna thought she might have risked it if she had been by herself, but she didn't think she could manage it with Jenny. From the water, the rock face down which they had jumped so easily would be impossible to climb with Jenny in her arms. Anna felt panic rising in her throat but it was important that Jenny shouldn't realize she was worried.

'Come on, Jenny,' she said. 'We'll find the next cave and shelter there until it stops raining.' She didn't say until the tide went down, though she had an idea that this would be necessary. And how long did tides take to go down? She had an awful feeling it might be twelve hours. And that would be the middle of the night. It was raining really hard now, and the tide as it came in was breaking furiously on the rocks so that it was difficult to tell what was rain and what was spray.

At last they came to the second cave. The pebbles at the front of it were wet, and at first Anna was scared to go in, realizing that this meant the tide reached its mouth and that if they crouched at the back of the cave they might be cut off completely in the darkness by a wall of water. But at this point the edge of the sea was still several yards away and she thought they had time to investigate, at any rate.

Anna switched on the torch and, holding Jenny's hand, walked into the cave.

'It goes on and on,' Jenny said. And it did. Unlike the first cave, this one seemed to twist right back upwards into the cliff.

'Just a minute,' Anna said. She put out the torch. 'Yes, I thought so. There's daylight ahead.' She had to crouch in the tunnel but Jenny could walk upright. Going on a bit farther, Anna found she could stand up, too. The tunnel had come out into a small round chamber and the daylight was coming from a large hole at the side of it. She climbed carefully out and found she was on a ledge, as wide as a table. It was covered with short grass. Anna wondered why the grass, never cut, never walked on, didn't grow long until it trailed over the edge of the ledge like green hair. Perhaps it was trodden by the feet of seagulls and stopped from flourishing by the wind.

She was high above sea level. The entrance to the cave and the rushing tide were below her. She felt the rain cold on her cheeks as she looked up. Above her was the cliff face, bare and rocky, with only odd tufts of grass and weeds growing in occasional pockets of earth. The top of the cliff was not very far away. The cliff face was about the height of a small house. But it might just as well have been the height of a skyscraper, Anna felt. It was far too steep for her to climb.

Jenny was begging to be allowed to see. Anna put her hand down and pulled Jenny up to join her. She liked feeling Jenny's hand in hers and was glad she wasn't alone.

It was still raining, and when she had seen what there was to see, Jenny was quite happy to go down into the dry cave again and 'play houses' with Anna. But first they took off their wet anoraks and put them on the ledge, weighted down with large stones from the floor of the cave. Jenny's anorak was bright red and would show up well, Anna thought, if anyone was looking for them. But who would be looking for them?

Their parents had gone out for the day, happily thinking Anna was looking after Jenny. Tears swam into Anna's eyes as she thought of this. How could she have been so stupid? How could she have brought Jenny into such a situation? Stephen wouldn't miss them, having lunch with his farm friends, not thinking or caring about what his sisters were doing.

Anna was glad Jenny couldn't see her tears. Jenny was busy in the semi-dark – the light from the hole lit only a small area – piling up stones to make a table. The stones were beautiful. Damp and glowing, it seemed as if they gave out a strange light of their own.

Anna put the packet of sandwiches on Jenny's 'table'. It was not smooth enough for the orange juice bottle, so she put that on the ground.

'What's in the sandwiches?' Jenny asked.

'Peanut butter in some. Ham in others.' They crouched in the dim, sandy, stony place and ate happily. Eating makes you feel a lot better.

'Treasure, measure, leisure, feasure, deasure,' Jenny said, when she'd finished her last mouthful. It was time for Anna to produce the treasure.

'I haven't even brought a spade,' Anna said, gloomily. 'I'm a hopeless treasure-hunter.' She had switched off the torch to save the battery, but now she switched it on again and bending down, went back along the tunnel to the sea. Although she had known it must happen, she didn't like seeing the low mouth of the cave full of water. There was only a narrow band of light between the sea and the rim of the cave. It widened and diminished as the tide retreated and advanced, as if some invisible hand were pulling it backwards and forwards. Strange reflections danced on the walls of the cave.

Jenny was just behind Anna and said, 'I don't like all that water. Where's the treasure?'

Anna shone the torch into every crevice in the walls of the cave. She moved some of the large, gleaming pebbles that lay on the floor of the cave and shone the torch into the round saucers of water that had lain beneath them.

Jenny was putting small stones in her pocket. 'Got my treasures,' she said.

They were certainly beautiful, these rounded veined stones, made smooth and silky by the action of the sea. Who had decided that gold and jewels were treasure and pebbles were not? Wet, they gleamed like jewels.

It was something to do with rarity and scarcity. No one really valued ordinary, commonplace things however beautiful they were. Scarlet pimpernels and pebbles might be as beautiful as gold but no one commented on them. It couldn't have been of them that Victoria Fisher was thinking when she wrote 'WATCH OUT FOR THE ONLY TREASURE'. And yet it was not of gold or jewels either. Anna was sure of that now, standing there in the strange light of the cave with the sound of the sea in her ears.

She brushed the sand off her clothes and ran her

hands through her hair. How messy Felicity would think her if she could see her now. She sighed, thinking of Felicity, immaculate on her immaculate horse. A cold wave splashing over her sandals brought Anna back to the present. She crouched down again and retreated into the inner cave.

Jenny was arranging her stones in patterns on the sandy floor. There seemed less light than ever. And all the time the tide rose higher, the water rushing into the cliff as if it were alive and keen to visit the most secret places.

EIGHT

Rescue

Stephen left *La Falaise* at about the same time that Anna and Jenny went down to the Hotel. He had promised he would be at the farm at ten. He was walking down the lane and wondering vaguely where his new friends were when they silently dropped down in front of him from trees on either side of the road – Denis, Yvonne, Marc and Gerard.

'You didn't see us, did you?' Denis asked.

'No,' Stephen admitted.

'Never let your Mum buy you a red sweater,' Yvonne said.

'Camouflage can be very useful,' Gerard added. 'You never know when you may need it.' He gave Marc a friendly punch in the ribs.

'Watch out, I've got Gingerbread,' Marc said, pulling the kitten out of his shirt front. 'Would you like to carry him, Stephen?'

Stephen looked at Denis, who nodded casually. The ginger kitten changed hands happily enough and settled down inside Stephen's shirt. It felt warm and tickled Stephen's bare skin.

'What are we doing today?' Gerard asked.

'I promised Dad we'd pick some tomatoes in the long field for an hour or two. He's got Mike off sick and he could do with a hand. Then I thought we'd have another go at rope-climbing.'

The five of them worked hard in the tomato field until their backs ached with the bending over. They had a little pile of split tomatoes that weren't good enough for sale.

'We'll cook those for lunch,' Denis said. 'But it's not time yet.'

They wandered over to the barn, stretching their backs by leaping into the air like Red Indians on the warpath. Stephen noticed there was a long rope hanging from an oak growing next to the barn. It was the same rope he had seen the children swinging on the morning before when he had walked up from the beach with his family, and envied them. Now he gave Gingerbread to Gerard and took hold of the rope and swung high into the air.

'See if you can climb it and get on to the barn roof,' Denis said.

'You first,' Stephen said.

The difficult part was getting on to the branch from the rope. Once astride the branch, holding on to another one above it, it was not too difficult to wriggle along and drop on to the flat barn roof.

They were all on top, even Gingerbread, who had come up in Gerard's shirt, when Denis and Yvonne's father came out and shouted to them.

'Denis! Yvonne! I'd like you to take a message to Mr Mesurier before lunch for me.'

They dropped down through a trapdoor in the barn roof into a hayloft and then down by a ladder to the floor. Their father wanted them to see if Mr Mesurier, who was retired and lived in a cottage on the cliff, would drive the boxes of tomatoes to the airport in place of the sick Mike. 'They've got to get there for the 4 o'clock plane,' the farmer said. 'And I've not got time to take them myself.'

Denis and Yvonne left Stephen, Gerard and Marc scrubbing potatoes in the farm kitchen and feeding Gingerbread with some scraps of kipper that had been left over from breakfast. It started to rain almost before the children were out of the farm gates, and they wished they had taken notice when their mother had shouted to them to put their anoraks on. But they didn't go back.

'It's all right,' Denis said. 'If you put your face up and welcome it. You can even drink it if you're thirsty.' They walked along the lane with their mouths open, feeling the raindrops on their tongues.

When they got to Mr Mesurier's cottage, the old man was having his dinner. Denis knocked. He called to them to come in. He wouldn't get up or stop eating but chased a pea round his plate with his fork while the children told him why they had come.

'Can't stand these frozen peas,' he said, munching happily. 'Tenderer than nature intended, but Mrs

Carter next door will cook 'em for me. Your Dad needs a bit of help, does he? Well, I'm not so old that I can't do a day's turn when I'm needed. Tell him I'll be along when I've finished my dinner. Sorry to hear that young Mike's took sick. I've not been sick myself in years.' There was certainly nothing wrong with his appetite. The children left him still eating.

'Let's go back along the cliff,' Yvonne said. 'We're so wet we can't get any wetter.'

As they walked along the track, Denis said 'The tide's very high. It must be just about on the turn.' He shivered and turned up the wet collar of his shirt. They hurried towards the Bay.

'Look, someone's left something by the side of the path,' Yvonne said, almost tripping over it. 'It's a pushchair. I suppose the people must have gone down on to the rocks. It seems odd in this weather.'

Denis dropped down himself to the rocks below the path. 'There's no sign of them.'

Yvonne was looking at the label. 'It says "Fisher" on it. That's funny. They're in England, and anyway, Simon's much too big for the pushchair now.'

'I expect Stephen's sisters borrowed it. I hope they know about the tides. It's coming in fast. I'll just have a look.' He went as far as he could but by this time the way was soon impassable.

Denis looked at Yvonne. He gulped. 'Let's go back along the cliff and see if we can see them from above.' They left the pushchair where it was and ran back the way they had come. It was raining quite hard now. Their soaked cotton shirts clung to their backs.

'Look there!' Yvonne saw the anoraks first. 'They must be in the second cave.' She called out but the wind was blowing in from the sea and it snatched her voice and threw it in the wrong direction.

It was then that they heard the sound of horses' hooves coming along the track from the Bay. The Horse Show was over and Felicity Le Brun, in smart white riding mack, was returning Dunbarton Star to the stables on the cliff.

Denis and Yvonne, lying full length on the grass at the edge of the cliff, gazing down at the anoraks, heard the horse stop and realized its rider must have seen the pushchair, too. Then the horse came on and almost galloped over them.

Denis suddenly knew what he must do. 'Stop!' he called to Felicity. 'There's some kids trapped by the tide. Can you go up to Fleuron Farm for us and get a rope?'

Felicity towered above them on the horse. 'Oh, they'll be all right,' she said. 'The tide never gets right up to the back of that cave. Dunbarton Star's had a long morning. I'm taking him back to the stable.' She felt guilty that she had not warned Anna about the tide. She didn't want to get involved. All her instincts made her want to get away and wipe the whole business right out of her mind. The wind whipped at the mane and tail of the horse.

Before she realized what was happening, Denis was hanging on to the reins and stopping her from leaving. How dared he? Who did he think he was to stop her doing what she wanted to do? Didn't Felicity Le Brun always get her own way? She had her riding crop in her left hand and brought it down across Denis's shoulders.

Denis's thin wet shirt gave him no protection and he squealed with the pain. Then anger flooded all over him like a warm bath.

'All right,' he grunted between closed teeth. 'You asked for it.' He gave her a violent push and, unprepared, she fell to the ground. The horse rose on its hind legs. Horse, boy, and girl were all on the very edge of the cliff, and for a moment it looked certain that one of them must plunge over. It seemed that only the force of the wind was driving them back. Yvonne, still on the ground, had covered her eyes, not daring to watch the fight.

And then it was over. Dunbarton Star's forelegs came down firmly on the path. Denis leapt into the saddle and was away.

The two girls looked at each other warily.

'It was your own fault,' Yvonne said. 'You should have helped.'

Felicity knew it was true. She said nothing. She got up slowly, feeling bruised and shaken, and looked down ruefully at her muddy riding mack.

'They'll be all right,' she said again. 'Please take Dunbarton Star back to the stables when you've

finished with him.' She walked off slowly down the path in the direction of the Hotel.

In the inner cave Jenny, her hands still clutching the beautiful pebbles, had gone to sleep with her head in Anna's lap. Anna, after feeling for ten minutes a horrified certainty that the probing tide would reach them in their farthest corner of the inner cave, had watched it slowly retreat, little by little, until it was safely back in the tunnel. It was all right, she thought, its chain was not long enough – the fierce animal could not harm them. Sure of this, she found herself slipping into sleep herself.

So she heard nothing when Yvonne called from the top of the cliff. So she heard nothing when boy and girl and horse fought on the edge of the cliff. And so she felt she was dreaming when, less than half an hour after that fight, she heard Denis's voice from the hole just above her.

He had tied his rope with one of his strongest knots to one of the bent pine trees that grew on the cliff top. With its help he was easily able to climb the twenty feet down to the narrow ledge above the inner cave. The rain had stopped but the wind still howled and the seagulls seemed to be crying out in amazement at the strange happenings on the cliff face.

They woke Jenny gently, helped her into her red anorak and persuaded her to climb on to Denis's back and hold on tightly to his neck. It was hard work but

there were footholds for his feet, and with his hands
climbing the rope he managed it. Yvonne had collected the pushchair while waiting for Denis and she
helped Jenny into it. Dunbarton Star stood there
patiently.

Denis went down the rope again and came up behind
Anna to give her confidence. Her legs felt leaden, and
her arms as if they were cotton wool. 'I'll never forget
about tides; I'll never forget about tides again.' The
words went over and over in her mind. 'I'm sorry,' she
said to Denis and Yvonne.

'Didn't you see the notice at the end of the road?'
Denis asked.

'*Many lives have been lost in this area. Do not venture
unless fully aware of tidal runs. Time and Tide wait for
no man.*' Denis and Yvonne said it together in sing-
song voices. They had learnt it off by heart.

'I'm sorry,' Anna said again.

Jenny just sucked her fingers.

There were baked potatoes and sausages and tomatoes for them in the warm, dry kitchen when they got
back to the farm.

'I had my lunch,' Jenny said, remembering sandwiches in the cave. 'It's like another day.'

'I don't want another day like this,' Anna said.

Next day was a different sort of day altogether. The
sun shone. It was difficult to believe there ever had been
wind and rain.

On their return Brenda and Luke Simpson had had to be told what had happened – though they were not told of Felicity's part in the day's adventures. They blamed themselves for having left the children alone for the day. They were, of course, very grateful to Denis and Yvonne and proposed to take them out for Sunday lunch as a way of saying thank you. There was only one good place for lunch near at hand – the Fleuron Bay Hotel.

So it was that the five Simpsons and the two de la Haye children sat over enormous icecreams on the hotel terrace. Fred muttered in Anna's ear as he passed, 'What happened yesterday, eh? I reckon Miss Felicity fell off her horse. Pride comes before a fall.'

There was no sign of Felicity. Anna ate her chocolate icecream slowly, to make it last as long as possible. Then she saw her. She was wearing white cotton trousers and a blue sailcloth jacket. There was a gleaming yacht at anchor in the bay, and a dinghy with a boy and girl in it was drawn up on the beach.

All the children watched Felicity run down the hotel steps, cross the road and join her friends by the dinghy on the beach, tossing her shining fair hair. Then Denis and Stephen and Luke Simpson started talking about the yacht. Yvonne helped Jenny count her pebbles which she had arranged in a semi-circle round her plate. Anna looked down at her hands. Only Brenda Simpson seemed delighted at the sight of the attractive girl.

Mrs Le Brun, Felicity's mother, came over to the table to make sure they had enjoyed their meal.

'It was delicious,' Brenda Simpson said. Then she nodded towards the beach where they could see Felicity in the dinghy, now being rowed out towards the yacht. 'And your daughter looks delicious, too. Anna is full of admiration for her.'

Mrs Le Brun gave a light laugh. 'Oh, Felicity, the darling. Yes, she's my only treasure.'

'*She's my only treasure.*' Anna heard the words and flushed. WATCH OUT FOR THE ONLY TREASURE. So that was what Victoria Fisher had meant. Anna scooped up the last remaining spoonful of icecream. 'All that glisters is not gold,' she thought, and smiled at Yvonne and Denis.

THE END